the perfect comeback of caroline jacobs

Matthew Dicks

ST. MARTIN'S GRIFFIN
NEW YORK

THE PERFECT COMEBACK OF CAROLINE JACOBS. Copyright © 2015 by Matthew Dicks.
All rights reserved. Printed in the United States of America. For information address
St. Martin's Press, 175 Fifth Avenue, New York, N.Y. 10010.

The Library of Congress has cataloged the hardcover edition as follows:

Dicks, Matthew.
    The perfect comeback of Caroline Jacobs : a novel / Matthew Dicks. — First edition.
        pages ; cm
    ISBN 978-1-250-00630-1 (hardcover)
    ISBN 978-1-4668-8632-2 (e-book)
    1. Mothers and daughters—Fiction.   2. Self-realization in women—Fiction.
3. Self-actualization (Psychology) in women—Fiction.   I. Title.
    PS3604.I323P47 2015
    813'.6—dc23

                                                                        2015017808

ISBN 978-1-250-11635-2 (trade paperback)

Our books may be purchased in bulk for promotional, educational,
or business use. Please contact your local bookseller or the
Macmillan Corporate and Premium Sales Department at 1-800-221-7945,
extension 5442, or by e-mail at MacmillanSpecialMarkets@macmillan.com.

First St. Martin's Griffin Edition: March 2017

10 9 8 7 6 5 4 3 2 1

*For Laura Marchand, my high school sweetheart
and the first person to ever believe in me.
The world deserved so much more of her light.*

one

Caroline Jacobs rose, pointed her finger at the woman seated at the center of the table reserved for the PTO president and her officers, and said it. Shouted it, in fact. In the cafeteria of Benjamin Banneker High School, surrounded by crowded bulletin boards, scuffed linoleum, and the lingering smell of chicken nuggets, Caroline Jacobs had shouted a four-letter word. *The* four-letter word.

The room fell silent.

This was the first time that Caroline had spoken up at a PTO meeting. It was the first time she had spoken publicly in any forum since high school, and the first time in her entire life that she had fired off an expletive in public. These were the thoughts racing through her mind as she looked across her trembling finger at the target of her scorn.

With that one word, Caroline Jacobs had been transformed, if only for an instant, into someone she was not. Someone entirely new. Someone she both wanted to be and never could be.

The silence that followed her outburst was filled with a palpable sense of discomfort. Several people turned their attention to the proposed budget, flipping through the stapled pages in an effort to avoid eye contact with either combatant. Eric Feeney, the father of twin girls and one of the few men in the room, bent over to tie his already tied sneakers. The women sitting beneath the "Race to the Top" bulletin board stopped knitting, their long needles frozen between stitches. Even the refrigerator silenced its thin rattle.

No one moved.

The woman to whom Caroline's four-letter word was directed, Mary Kate Dinali, recovered quickly, converting her initial reaction of shock into a prefabricated facade of disgust and condescension.

Caroline wasn't surprised. Mary Kate Dinali was well equipped for this sort of verbal combat. She had spent her entire life conquering sidewalk fiefdoms, forging parental alliances, and coalescing suburban power. This was her life's work. She was a master in the art of indignation and passive-aggressive backstabbing. She was a Navy SEAL of PTO politics. And Caroline, without weapon or training of any kind, had just stepped onto the field of battle. She had opened fire on a hardened veteran of many skirmishes, and while her accusation had been leveled with uncommon force and precision, it had bounced off her opponent's armor like paperclips shot from an elastic band.

Mary Kate—now fully recovered and back in control—rose slowly from her seat, her thin waistline and cashmere twinset on full display.

Standing up was good, Caroline thought. She wished she had thought of it first.

Instead, she was unable to move, frozen in place by the eyes of more than three dozen people who were shifting glances from Caroline to Mary Kate and back, awaiting their next move.

But Caroline had no next move. Her actions had been as much a surprise to her as they had been to everyone else. She had nothing left in her repertoire.

In truth, Caroline Jacobs had no repertoire.

Tom Jacobs rose from his seat and placed his arm around his wife's shoulders. "Maybe we'll just head home a little early," he said, giving her a gentle nudge.

Caroline still didn't move. Not immediately, anyway. Part of her appreciated Tom's attempt to extricate her from this disaster, but she didn't like the tone of his voice. Rather than sounding earnest or concerned, his statement had come across as . . . relaxed. Yes, that was it. There was a nonchalant quality to his statement, a *Whoa, where did that come from, little lady?* tenor that she didn't like one bit. It was the voice of a man with a foot in each camp, a man who was straddling the fence separating opponents.

At this moment, Caroline didn't require the delicacies of fence-straddling. She needed her husband fully on her side. She was already regretting her outburst. And that's exactly what it had been. An outburst. An unexpected verbal explosion. A sudden loss of control brought on by a brief but unquestionable moment of insanity.

She didn't need Tom coming down on the side of crazy as well. Not even halfway.

Nevertheless, she was grateful to him for conquering her inertia. She took his hand and a few tentative steps, but not before flashing him a glare, perfected during years of marriage, that conveyed a clear and pointed message. She dipped her head and stared at the tiled floor as they walked past Mary Kate and her PTO storm troopers. She cursed her inability to find a second sentence to follow the first. She hated herself for even saying the first.

Once they were clear of the school's double doors, Tom released her hand. "What was that?" he asked in a low voice.

For once, Caroline wished her husband would have used his own four-letter word—if not that very same f-word, something with equal force. Something other than his standard, modulated caution. But four-letter words were not in Tom's repertoire either.

"What was that?" Caroline shot back. "You heard Mary Kate. You heard what she said."

"I didn't hear anything that deserved a response like that."

"Then you weren't listening." She opened the passenger door to the minivan and climbed in.

Tom entered on the driver's side and started the ignition. Just as he was about to resume the conversation, press his initial point, perhaps approach it from another angle—all the things that he did so well—Caroline interjected.

"I don't want to talk about it right now. Okay? Let's just go home."

The gag order would frustrate Tom, and she was glad.

Mary Kate Dinali had it coming. Of this Caroline was certain. She only wondered why someone hadn't let her have it years before. The fact that it was Caroline who had said it—quiet, obedient, always ready to help, never rocking the boat Caroline Jacobs— had probably come close to knocking several of the PTO old-timers off their cafeteria stools and onto the floor.

To an outsider who wasn't paying close attention to the pro- ceedings, Caroline's outburst might have seemed unwarranted. But context was essential. Mary Kate had just moved the discussion from next month's school fair to an item on the agenda that she had titled "The Spirit of Volunteerism."

"This is going to be a quick item," she'd said. "No biggie."

Like most bullies, Mary Kate Dinali liked to sneak up on her victims. Surprise them with false kindness, or in this case, misdi- rection. Before launching into the agenda item, she had smiled at Eric Feeney, who smiled back. He was wearing a New York Gi- ants jersey, an intentional reminder to everyone present that the NFL now played games on Thursday nights. "I know the game starts in twenty minutes," Mary Kate said. "And people need to get home in time for kickoff."

Eric Feeney laughed. She had him, and with him, she had the rest. Just like that.

"As you know," Mary Kate continued, "our Election Day bake sale was a huge success, and our Feed the Teachers campaign was probably our best ever. How many schools offer their teachers sushi rolls and cappuccinos during parent-teacher conferences? In fact, I can't remember the last time we had a bad event. But here's the thing, friends: At both of these events, and at most of our events last year and the year before that, I see the same faces. The same people are giving their all, while so many others are sitting on the sidelines, relying on the good work of just a few of us to carry the day."

Caroline was already seething by the time Mary Kate had come to the end of what sounded like a well-rehearsed speech, but Mary Kate had been equally condescending on any number of occasions in the past. This was nothing new. Par for the course.

Then Jessica Trent spoke.

"It's not easy for some of us," Jessica said, her voice wavering. Jessica Trent was a thin, freckled redhead who had more fire in her hair than her demeanor. Caroline had spoken to the mother of two on several occasions, but being that she and Jessica were both fairly shy, they hadn't managed to connect. Shy people, in Caroline's experience, rarely forge successful friendships because they need an extrovert to make things happen. Someone to take the first step, make the first phone call, and assume the initial risk. Shy people like Caroline and Jessica require a facilitator of sorts to get things started, and there had been no one to bring the women together.

It was a shame. Caroline suspected that she and Jessica Trent had a lot in common. She was a smart woman who possessed a dry humor that Caroline appreciated. Her children were well be-haved. She might speak as infrequently as Caroline at the PTO meetings, but in the few times that Caroline had heard Jessica talk to her kids, she had been direct and assertive. Funny, even.

But as she spoke now, Jessica's voice had an unusual bite, an edge that seemed to come more from anger than nerves. Jessica Trent didn't like Mary Kate's condescending tone, either, but unlike Caroline, she was willing to speak up about it. "I have to pay a baby-sitter just to come to these meetings," Jessica said. "And it's not like I can just leave work in the middle of the day to come to the school to help out."

"I had to hire a babysitter, too," Mary Kate said. "So did Pauline," she added, gesturing to the blond, bangled woman to her right. "I'm guessing that a lot of people here tonight had to do the same. We're all making sacrifices, and we certainly appreciate yours, Jess. I just worry that some are sacrificing more than their fair share."

What Mary Kate didn't say—what she didn't need to say since everyone in the room already knew perfectly well—was that she and Pauline needed babysitters tonight because their husbands were in Myrtle Beach on their biannual golf outing.

Jessica Trent's husband was a security guard in a downtown parking garage.

"I'm not saying that some aren't helping more than others," Jessica said. "Just that people might already be helping as much as they can, given their circumstances."

"I'm sure that's the case for some," Mary Kate said. "And I don't want this to go on too long or sound combative. I'm just saying that in the spirit of volunteerism, perhaps you should all ask yourselves if you could be doing more. And if you can't, at least offer a word or two of thanks to the people in the room who are bearing the heaviest loads. A little appreciation can go a long way. That's all. But thank you for the feedback, Jessica. Appreciated as always."

Mary Kate looked down at the agenda, ready to move on, when Jessica spoke again. "You're looking for a thank-you?"

"Excuse me?" Mary Kate asked.

"You want us to thank you?"

"No," Mary Kate said, dismissing the notion with a wave of her hand. "I was just saying that some people might be doing a lot, and I worry that they may feel a little underappreciated."

At this, Pauline cleared her throat. "If you're the first to arrive and the last to leave at every event, you start to wonder where everyone else is."

"But I also understand that it's beyond some people's means to do more," Mary Kate said. "I get that. We all have our own personal struggles. But giving a little more might not be beyond the reach for everyone. And we could at least make sure that those who are able to help out the most feel appreciated for the time that they give. It's not easy for any of us. I know. This is hard work."

"Yes, it is," Pauline said.

The five women flanking Mary Kate nodded.

Caroline's gaze shifted to Jessica, who looked small and alone. "Sure," she said, her head hanging a little bit lower than before. "I just don't want anyone feeling bad about not being able to do more. Some people might not seem to be giving a lot, but they might be giving more than you could imagine. I'd hate for them to feel bad for not doing more—"

"Well, you know what Eleanor Roosevelt said," Mary Kate cut in. "No one can make you feel inferior without your consent."

Pauline nodded.

Jessica appeared to shrink on her stool. Her hands came together on her lap, like a scolded schoolgirl.

"Wouldn't you agree, Jessica?" Mary Kate asked.

That's when Caroline rose from her seat. That was when she lost her composure. That was when Caroline Jacobs said *fuck*.

By the time she and Tom were pulling into the driveway, Caroline was weighing her options. She knew she needed a strategy. *Damage control,* Tom would call it. It would require a formal letter of apology to the PTO for her "unfortunate, regrettable, and inappropriate language." Probably a personal apology as well. Caroline could do that. She could muster a face-to-face *I'm sorry* without much trouble. She'd been doing passive, disingenuous things all her life. What was one more?

It was true. *Passive* was the word that described Caroline best. It was almost her way of life. Avoid conflict at all costs. Be aggressively agreeable whenever possible. Fly under the radar. Don't stir the pot. Acquiesce and move on from difficult situations as quickly as possible, preferably with a smile. These were her mantras. Even her job as a photographer placed Caroline in a passive position, behind the lens, out of the shot, far away from the scene.

Lift the camera, peer through the viewfinder, and be instantly transported from any uncomfortable moment to a tiny, encapsulated world. Caroline had been doing this her entire life. Dodging and weaving. Ducking and disengaging. Anything to go unnoticed. Unseen.

But now something else was happening that she didn't quite understand. There was something in the pit of her stomach that she had never felt before. Smoldering embers that had been waiting to be lit for years.

Fire.

Caroline knew that she should apologize. She knew that she would apologize. But a part of her was rebelling against this notion. Part of her—a new part—was almost refusing to even consider an apology. Part of her was still reveling in that PTO moment.

Tonight's events, and the confluence of circumstances that had led up to them, had ignited a fire within her that she didn't think possible. Yes, it was only a flicker, not quite a flame. Nevertheless Caroline suspected that it wouldn't take much for it to burst into a roaring bonfire. She could feel it right there, just waiting to ignite.

She wasn't sure if she should be excited or terrified by the prospect.

two

"Do you want to talk about it?" Tom asked, pulling back the curtains and letting sunlight fall upon the bed. Caroline turned away.

"Not now," she said. "Okay?"

Okay. Caroline had been using that word, phrased as a question, as a means of garnering approval for most of her life. It had become a habit of sorts—her mother had pointed it out on more than one occasion—and though it had never really bothered her, the word suddenly felt rotten in her mouth.

For the first time in her life, it felt wrong.

"I'll see you later then," Tom said. He leaned over and kissed her. "Have a good morning."

As she brushed her teeth and pulled her dark hair back into a ponytail, Caroline's thoughts returned to the events of the previous evening. It had been ages since she had allowed her emotions to get the best of her. She honestly couldn't remember the last time. This was in large part due to her desire to avoid or diminish any situation where she or anyone else might become emotional. Caroline specialized in the suffering of tiny indignities in silence. Not complaining when the woman in the drive-thru handed her a three-quarters-filled cup of coffee. Pretending not to notice when someone cut in front of her at the pharmacy. Never once sending a single food item back at a single restaurant for fear of upsetting . . . well, anybody.

But there were big things, too. Like agreeing with Tom to have only one child when their original plan was for two. Deciding not to open a photography studio even though she always dreamed of a place of her own. Allowing people like Mary Kate Dinali to walk all over her.

Maybe all of this had finally led her to a breaking point. Maybe she had simply uttered one too many *Okay?*s

Pushing these thoughts aside, Caroline donned a robe and headed down to breakfast. Her heart sank halfway down the staircase at the tinkle of silver on porcelain coming from the kitchen. This was immediately followed by shame.

Disappointment at having to face your daughter this early in the morning was bad enough. Dreading any and all contact with your daughter was almost unbearable. No, it *was* unbearable. What kind of mother tried to avoid her child at all costs? But this is where Caroline's relationship with her daughter currently stood: mutually intolerable tolerance.

Through spits and spats and bits and bites, their relationship had devolved into a permanent state of détente in which both parties avoided conflict at all costs. In many ways, Caroline no longer thought of herself as a mother, but more of a caretaker. Someone responsible for her daughter's safety and upkeep, but little else. It didn't help that Tom had somehow maintained peace with their daughter while a cold war raged around him. Caroline was happy that Polly could turn to her father in times of need, but she resented his ability to remain in good standing with their daughter when she could not.

Caroline forced a smile upon her face and entered the kitchen with as much spring in her step as she could muster. This morning would be different. If she could tell Mary Kate Dinali to fuck off, she could handle her own daughter, goddamn it.

"Morning!" she said.

Polly was sitting at the kitchen table, head hanging low over a textbook as she hoisted Frosted Flakes to her mouth from a plastic bowl. She was wearing a shirt that Caroline did not like—but this was not uncommon given her daughter's vast and unusual T-shirt collection. This morning's tee was black and white with the images of a seal, a manatee, and a panda lined across the chest. The words above the images read:

THIS SHIRT IS 100% ORGANIC.
65% BABY SEAL. 20% MANATEE. 15% PANDA.
ALL DELICIOUS AND NUTRITIOUS.

Caroline had found the shirt mildly amusing when she first saw it, but that was before Polly began wearing it, and others like it, to church functions, school concerts, and the recent statewide high school debate, where she had placed a surprising second.

The only thing the shirt had going for it, in Caroline's opinion, was that it suited the image that her daughter had carefully crafted for herself perfectly: cropped hair that looked as though it had been cut with garden shears; an eyebrow ring and stud in her nose (neither one parentally approved); blue jeans covered in ink drawings; a tattoo of the ace of spades on the small of her back that Polly had yet to mention and Caroline had yet to acknowledge.

And T-shirts. Lots and lots of T-shirts. All of them emblazoned with sentiments just as sarcastic and snarky as this one.

Caroline had confided in her closest friend, Wendy, that she thought her daughter was becoming a Goth but had been immediately corrected. "She's not Goth. She's punk."

Wendy explained that Goth was worse but temporary. More of a phase than an actual lifestyle choice. Goths were sullen and detached. "Purposefully disinterested," Wendy said, which could be incredibly annoying but almost impossible to pull off for very long. "You can't not care about anything for only so long."

"Punk," she had said by way of comparison, "was a way of life." It represented anger and nonconformity, but punk was still employable. Dateable. Relatable even to the nonpunk. Punk had earned some respect in the world. Punk was slightly mainstream.

"Polly is definitely punk."

Caroline was not consoled.

When Polly didn't respond to her greeting, Caroline almost let it go, opting to preserve the peace of the morning over the platitudes and pleasantries of proper parenting. Why pick a fight when one could be avoided? On any other morning she would have done exactly that, happy to escape without a full-blown argument. But on this day, Caroline was determined not to let her sleeping-dog-of-a-daughter lie. A mingling of desire to do the right thing, along with an inexplicable willingness to embrace potential conflict, forced her to speak.

"Hey!" she said, trying to maintain a tone of cheeriness. "When someone says good morning, it's nice to say something back."

Polly's spoon paused on its arc to her mouth. With her head still buried in her textbook, she said, "Did you know that shrapnel was named after its inventor?"

"What?"

Polly sighed. It was one of the things that she did best. She had elevated the sigh to an art form.

"A guy named Henry Shrapnel invented shrapnel," Polly said. "You know. The stuff that kills you when a bomb explodes. It was named after him. Crazy, huh? Kind of like if mustard gas was named after Colonel Mustard. Except it wasn't. But wouldn't it be great if it was?"

"Sure," Caroline said.

"And I thought George Washington had it bad for having that freakin' bridge named after him," Polly added through a Frosted Flake mumble.

"You're studying history?" Caroline asked.

"No. Chemistry. I'm not even taking history this semester. Geez, Mom."

"Chemistry?"

Polly sighed again. "That's what I said."

"Need any help?" she asked, pouring coffee from the pot that Polly had brewed for herself earlier this morning. A reminder of a dietary battle lost last year.

"Not unless you can explain the noble gases to me in the next three minutes," Polly said. "I wish you'd let me study."

"I know a lot about the noble gases. I'm practically an expert on noble gases. But nothing I could explain in just three minutes." She smiled, hoping for one in return.

"Right," Polly said, and stuffed another spoonful of cereal into her mouth.

Caroline took a seat across from her daughter, realizing that Polly had yet to even look at her. "I know you don't believe it, but there will come a day when you and I won't see each other very much. You'll be off living your life somewhere, and we're going to regret not spending more time together when you were young."

"I believe it," Polly said, still not looking up. "At least the part about not seeing each other every day. I sure as hell don't plan on living here forever."

"You'd be surprised how quickly things can change."

Polly finally looked up. "I'm fifteen, Mom. I'm not stupid. I get the whole time flies thing. It's flying by right now." Polly looked up at the clock and winced. "Fuck, I got to go."

It hadn't been a great conversation, but at least it had been something. Caroline didn't want to ruin it by bringing up the rule about swearing. Besides, she was hardly one to be making speeches about the use of four-letter words. She remained silent as Polly rose from the table, slung a backpack over her shoulder, tucked the chemistry textbook under an arm, and left the house without another word.

Polly's cereal bowl, half filled with milk, was still on the table. Her spoon lay beside it in a small white puddle.

three

The spider had apparently finished with her web for the day. Either that or she'd decided to take a much-deserved break. The gossamer threads stretched from the edge of the brick windowsill over to a teetering shelf, then across to an ancient, wooden stool, where they formed a tiny trampoline of sorts. Charlotte, the admittedly less-than-creative name that Caroline had given the small, black creature, was nestled in the corner of her web, her legs hidden beneath her bulbous body. It wasn't the best place for the spider in terms of composition, but this project had become more about web and light than spider. Lying on her back beneath the web in what seemed like the dust of a thousand years, Caroline pointed her Nikon upward, waiting for the first ray of sunlight to knife through the broken window above.

Right on schedule, at four minutes before 9:00 A.M., the single yellow ray appeared, reflecting off dust particles suspended in the air before cutting through the spider's web. Caroline held her breath and depressed the shutter button, capturing her first image of the day. This vast room had once been the home to many men and machines, but now the silence was broken only by the click and whir of the camera. Caroline fired off about twenty shots before the single ray of light had blossomed into a warm, gauzy glow.

She stood and inspected the images using the small screen on the back of the camera. She was pleased. After a moment of scrolling between them, Caroline narrowed her choices down to three. She would make the final decision when she saw them on a larger screen at home.

What now? Wait to see if Charlotte became ambitious again? Hope to catch her in the middle of a meal? Finish off this project with today's image and move onto something else? She didn't need to decide now. She would be back tomorrow. She'd let Charlotte decide.

Caroline turned and crossed the enormous space, picking her way between overturned tables, rusted machines, and crumbling brick pillars. She was trespassing in this abandoned factory, as she'd been doing every day for more than a year, but she had begun to think of this space as her own. Her workshop. The studio she had always wanted.

In truth, she felt this way about a lot of abandoned buildings that she visited—an even dozen in her current rotation—though this was the only one she visited daily. It was close to home, easy to enter, and most important, the light was spectacular. The windows were boarded up in many of the mills and warehouses where she worked. But this factory, which once produced shoes, leather bags, and dressage saddles, still had many of its windows intact—including two rows of rectangular windows at the top of the vaulted ceiling. In another ten minutes, the sunlight would strike those windows, sending a cataract of fiery rays down upon the factory floor. No matter how many times Caroline returned to this place, she always found something new to shoot. Decrepit furniture and machinery made beautiful by the right combination of sunlight, dust, and age. Frozen gears and idle chains that had not moved for decades. Cracked, dirt-smeared glass capturing the light in new and seemingly impossible ways.

And best of all, the creatures that had taken up residence in these abandoned places. Charlotte and her insect brethren. Birds. Squirrels. Bats. Mice. Even rats made for some of her most interesting subjects. Caroline had once managed to capture the image of a rat mother feeding her tiny, pink babies as the slanting sunlight made her eyes sparkle gold. Even Tom, who didn't have an appreciation for anything that wasn't presented in the written form, had found great beauty in that photograph. He had gasped when she showed it to him. At first, she thought his reaction was to the rats themselves.

"I know they're rats," she had said. "But they're—"

"Beautiful," Tom, had said, finishing her sentence. "Look at them. Look at her," he said, running his index finger over the image of the rat mother's whiskers, which had picked up flecks of sunlight. "You made her look . . . glorious."

"You think?"

"I know that rats are God's creatures," Tom had said. "But until now, I don't think I ever really believed that. I mean . . . just look at them."

That had been a very good day.

Despite Tom's reaction, Caroline was hesitant to show him or anyone else her work. Tom was encouraging and tried to offer feedback, but he simply wasn't equipped to appreciate what she was doing. He liked her work, but he didn't know how to express his opinions clearly.

Or maybe he only liked her work because he was married to the photographer.

Caroline's college classmates had been almost desperate for attention, willing to plaster their images on any wall they could find. Their thirst for eyeballs was insatiable, but to Caroline, these public displays were terrifying. Heartrending. Offering her work to the world required a level of courage that she couldn't muster. I work for myself, she had tried to convince herself for the past ten years. She imagined herself as the novelist who refused to share her masterpiece with anyone until it was complete.

She was simply waiting for her first masterpiece.

But she had also fantasized about presenting at a local art show under an assumed name. Maybe even visiting the show and listening in to what people would say about her work. The idea appealed to her. She craved the combination of honesty and anonymity that only a fly on the wall could enjoy: the ability to both receive and hide from the possible criticism. In the end, though, a pseudonym would only protect her identity. The rejection (and it was rejection she feared), would still fall squarely on her shoulders, pseudonym or not.

But this project, beginning with the first version of Charlotte's web three weeks ago, was the best work that she had ever done. No doubt. She felt prouder of these images than any she had ever captured before, and with that pride came a glimmer of confidence that she rarely felt. Not enough to pitch the series to a local museum or an art show, but enough to show Tom and maybe even Wendy or her cousin Julie. Maybe even Polly. See what they thought.

Maybe.

four

There were days when Caroline wished that Tom had taken a job with a firm after he graduated from law school. He'd had plenty of offers. And he had enough student debt to choke a horse. They both did. An attorney's salary would've gone a long way to cover what they were still paying back twenty years later. It also would've meant that the health insurance Caroline's job afforded them wouldn't be so critical to the family's well-being.

Nevertheless, Tom had decided to hang up his own shingle. He worked hard for almost ten years before the practice finally went under, partly because the economy collapsed, partly because of the fierce competition, but mostly because Tom was an excellent attorney and a less-than-excellent businessman. By the time he was forced to admit that he couldn't make it on his own, the offers from the larger firms had evaporated as younger, hungrier law school graduates filled the few positions available.

At thirty-five, he was an old man in the eyes of the big firms.

But then there were mornings like this one when Caroline was glad that Tom had decided to forgo a career in corporate law and the enormous time commitment that it would have required. Sure, their fixer-upper farmhouse was more of a fixer-upper today than when they bought it. And Caroline's Subaru was almost as old as their teenage daughter. And they hadn't been on a real vacation since they had taken Polly to Disney when she was six. But they had the freedom of days like these, when Tom could meet with her for breakfast without worrying about rushing off to a court date or clawing through a pile of paperwork or making partner. Though he would've made an excellent corporate attorney, the law would've taken Tom away from Caroline and Polly far too often for both their liking.

When his business finally went under, Tom continued to practice law on the side whenever he could while starting a house-painting business (something he had done while in college), and later adding replacement window sales and installation to supplement his income. He liked working with his hands. He enjoyed the freedom that came with owning his business, and unlike the complexities of a law practice, this business was simple.

Paint a house. Collect payment. Repeat.

It wasn't a long-term plan, but it was a way to pay back the debt that his business had incurred. Plus, Tom liked the work.

Then, about a year after launching his painting business, the ramshackle church that they attended (and that Tom had recently painted free of charge) was in need of a new deacon. The minister asked Tom if he would like the job. He was surprised by the offer. In the ten years that the Jacobs family had been members of the church, Tom had helped out whenever possible, but he had hardly been on a leadership track. Besides, he had no formal training as a deacon and barely understood the job. These turned out to be small hurdles to overcome. The aging minister had a good feeling about Tom. The congregation trusted him. It wouldn't hurt to have an attorney working for the church, either. And unlike passing the bar, there was no test in order to become a church deacon. No official requirements. Tom could learn on the job and collect a small paycheck to add to his collection of small paychecks.

Tom and Caroline had discussed the possibility of Tom becoming more involved with the church over a dinner of macaroni and cheese and peas. She remembered the conversation well. Tom had been more excited about this job than any other in his life, and the schedule would still afford him the freedom that he now prized. Caroline was proud of Tom for the trust and responsibility that the church was willing to offer him, but she was envious, too. Someone had noticed him. Without any real effort on his part, someone had recognized his talent and tapped him for something important.

Caroline was still waiting for someone to notice her talent.

In the end, the church turned out to be a true calling for her husband. He wasn't the most devout man in the church (Caroline sometimes wondered if he even believed in God), and he wasn't the most knowledgeable in terms of Scripture, but Tom was a natural leader whom people wanted to follow. A year after becoming deacon, Tom was asked to launch an adult Bible study program and become one of the program's first teachers. A year after that, he began counseling congregants on issues ranging from marital problems to substance abuse. He found that he was surprisingly adept at helping people solve their problems or leading them to people more capable than himself.

He still sold replacement windows and painted homes, hiring college kids in the summer when business occasionally boomed. He had also become a notary and a justice of the peace, officiating weddings when the minister was unavailable and even for couples who weren't affiliated with the church. Anything to bring in a little more money. "I do a little bit of this and a little bit of that," he would tell people when asked about his occupation, and it was true. So what if money was almost always tight? They were almost always happy.

Today they were meeting in the rose garden in William Wynne Memorial Park. Caroline found Tom sitting on the south end of the garden on a flannel blanket beside a picnic basket, a book in hand.

"Reading Scripture?" she asked, knowing he was not.

"Sort of," he said, holding up the book. "The Steve Jobs biography. A story of redemption."

"If you're not an ass, you don't require redemption."

Tom laughed. "How'd it go?"

"Good," she said, sitting beside him. "Pretty great, actually."

"Lots of creepy crawlies?"

"Just one."

"The spider?" he asked.

"Yup."

"I still don't understand why you don't shoot here. Look at this place." He pointed to the rosebushes, which formed an intricate series of paths that led to a central gazebo.

"Everyone shoots here."

"Everyone shoots here because it's beautiful," Tom said.

"So is Charlotte, if I shoot her right."

"Can I see her?" Tom asked.

"I didn't shoot her today," Caroline said. "Just the web."

"Didn't look her best?"

"Something like that," she said, smiling. "I'll print a few at work today and show you tonight."

Tom opened up the picnic basket beside him and removed a thermos of coffee and two ceramic mugs. He poured steaming coffee into both and added sugar to his. He handed the cup to Caroline and raised his own. "To ugly spiders made beautiful."

They clinked mugs.

As Caroline sipped her coffee, Tom removed bagels and bananas from the basket.

They ate in silence for a couple of minutes, watching the runners, dog walkers, and mothers with strollers make their way around them.

It wasn't unusual for the two of them to sit like this, still and at ease. Tom lived much of his life inside his head, constantly juggling his many hats. She often thought that a giraffe could walk by and he wouldn't notice. Moreover, Tom was careless and lacked attention to detail. It was one of the primary reasons that his law practice went under. When Caroline first met him, Tom's bank account was a disaster. He would forget to deposit checks and his account would be constantly overdrawn. He'd forget to return phone calls. And his bachelor diet had consisted mainly of Pop-Tarts, bananas, and coffee.

Caroline, on the other hand, approached the world at a safe distance. She was an observer. A watcher. A master of fine print. She noticed detail and subtle change. She preferred the small to the large, the background to the foreground. She dotted every *i* and crossed every *t*. She balanced her checkbook to the penny (back when people actually did this) and scheduled her day into thirty-minute increments. She researched before making any purchase, visited the dentist twice a year, and checked for lumps once a month.

Tom and Caroline balanced each other perfectly. They were comfortable with each other, even in their silence. But today's silence felt less than comfortable. They had yet to speak about the PTO meeting, and though Caroline would've been more than willing to avoid the subject for a little longer (if not altogether), she was sure that Tom would not. He was not a man who avoided conflict. He did not allow sleeping dogs to ever lie.

He was pouring a second cup of coffee from the thermos when he finally asked, "So are you feeling okay after last night?"

"I'm fine."

"What do you plan on doing?" he asked.

"I don't know. What do you think Mary Kate's planning on doing?"

Tom paused a moment before responding. He was surprised by her question. She'd surprised herself, too.

"I'm not saying that Mary Kate wasn't wrong," he said. "But you did sort of escalate things."

"Just because she didn't drop any f-bombs doesn't mean she wasn't escalating things. You don't get a free pass just because you're a passive-aggressive bitch. You can't treat people the way she treated Jessica and get away with it."

"I agree," he said. "I was just wondering if you planned on doing anything."

He sounded like Tom the Counselor, and it annoyed the hell out of her. She knew he couldn't help it. A thousand counseling sessions on a thousand living room couches had left him sounding mechanical in conversations like these. Clinical, almost. Caroline could admire Tom's equanimity when he used it to help other people, but when he used it on her, consciously or otherwise, she despised it.

"I don't know what I'll do yet," she said. "I might do nothing."

"I'll support you either way," Tom said.

She knew that he meant it. Tom had never lied to her, and she loved him for it. She hated him for it too, because she knew that his utter lack of subterfuge was the result of an unwavering belief that his intentions were noble in almost everything he did. "My results might not be great," he often said, "but my intentions are good."

"Did you know that it was Lucy's anniversary yesterday?" he asked.

Now it was Caroline's turn to be surprised. "You thought I forgot?"

"No, but you usually mention it. I was just wondering if that might've been part of it. Maybe you were upset already?"

"Maybe," she said.

There was no maybe about it.

Caroline rarely lied to her husband. She might tell a small, white lie from time to time. She might stretch the truth on occasion. But she would never lie about anything significant. Except when it came to Lucy. Almost everything she had ever said to her husband about Lucy had been a lie. This, too.

five

Caroline was in her customary place, wedged between the exterior wall of the Sears Portrait Studio and the hedgerow that lined the front of the building. She was crouched between two large shrubs, her camera lens filling a small gap between the greenery that looked out onto the parking lot. Branches poked at her from all angles, but she ignored them and focused directly ahead. The van had just entered the parking lot and was pulling into the spot closest to the building. She raised her camera and prepared to shoot.

A thin woman with dreadlocks and a brightly colored head-scarf stepped out of the van and made her way to the passenger door just as the chime on the studio door sounded. Caroline turned to her left and watched as Henry Parker, a middle-aged man carrying a pet carrier in each hand, pulled the door open and stepped inside.

She hoped Henry would wait patiently.

She knew it was unlikely.

Caroline turned back toward the parking lot and refocused her camera on the woman by the van. She began to shoot, switching from wide angles to close-ups, focusing and firing as quickly as possible. A minute later, the woman had locked her van and was pushing a wheelchair-bound girl across the parking lot and through the same door Henry Parker had entered just moments before. She waited another moment, to be sure that the woman wouldn't see her emerge from the bushes. She counted to ten.

Then it was time to go. Hurry up, in fact, before Henry becomes . . . Henry. She wished she could stay hidden behind the bush until Tiffany arrived, and she was a little annoyed about being left alone.

But only a little.

Caroline didn't begrudge her coworker's tardiness. For Tiffany, this was just a job. Not a career.

This made it all the more painful for Caroline, knowing that she had graduated from Providence College with a degree in photography, and yet she and Tiffany were doing exactly the same job. And Tiffany did it better.

It wasn't that Tiffany's photographs were superior to Caroline's. At Sears Portrait Studio, there was no room for creativity; any attempt to infuse a personal touch or an exacting eye was frowned upon. Standard portraits were taken at standard angles at standard distances with standard backgrounds. Every shot was prescribed. That was the essence of the Sears Portrait Studio experience. The actual photography involved could have been done by almost anybody. But Tiffany possessed an innate ability to handle the difficult customer in a way that Caroline did not. The studio was a breeding ground for difficult customers. Henry Parker was one of them. And now he was being kept waiting.

Henry was the only customer in her twelve years on the job who Caroline could describe as a regular. He was as close to a crazy old cat lady as a fastidious, obsessive-compulsive cat lover in his early forties could get: a little odd, but not exactly certifiable.

But like a crazy old cat lady, Henry Parker owned cats. A great number of cats. More cats than any human being should ever own. Once a month he arrived promptly at the studio for his standing appointment with an assortment of feline friends.

Since Henry was relatively benign if handled promptly, Caroline took care of almost all his shoots. She could deal with cats. Actually, she was excellent with cats. Cats and rats and spiders. Anything with more than two legs was her specialty. It was the human beings who caused Caroline the most trouble.

But now she was keeping Henry waiting. She needed to extract herself from behind these bushes and move.

When she entered the lobby, Henry was standing at the counter, tapping his foot both dramatically and impatiently.

"Hi, Henry."

"There you are," he said, spinning around. "Geez, I could've stolen the cash register, and no one would've been the wiser."

"So you're a felon now, are you?"

Henry stared, blank faced. It reminded Caroline a little bit of Polly's rehearsed indifference.

"Sorry," she continued. "I had to step out for a second. I wasn't far. Besides, that cash register is heavy. I would've caught you."

"You're the only one working today?" he asked, motioning in the direction of Mrs. Arnold, who was sitting beside her daughter's wheelchair. "I don't want to be rushed. You know this takes time."

"I know," Caroline said. "Tiffany's coming in. She's just running late."

Henry shook his head disapprovingly. "Not exactly running a tight ship today."

"She'll be here in a minute." Caroline turned her back to Henry. She knew he was only getting warmed up. "Mrs. Arnold?"

"Yes," she said, rising from her seat. Mrs. Arnold was a tall, dark-skinned woman with large, brown eyes and perfect teeth. She spoke with an accent. Jamaican, maybe? Haitian? Caroline wasn't sure. "And this is my daughter, Alysha," she said, motioning to the girl in the wheelchair.

Alysha was about ten years old and was severely handicapped. Her head and neck were held up in a cushioned support column, and she appeared to have little control over her arms. Cerebral palsy, her mother explained when she had made the appointment. The girl offered Caroline a haphazard wave and uttered something like "Hello."

"Hi, Alysha. I'm Caroline." She returned the wave. "Sorry I was late, Mrs. Arnold. I'll get you in the studio in just a minute."

"You're right on time," she said. "Don't worry a bit."

"Wait—you're taking her first?" Henry asked. "That means I'll be stuck with Tiffany. No way am I letting her shoot my cats. Do you have any idea what she did to Felonious Monk the last time I let her near my baby?"

"Can you work with me here, Henry? I just need a few minutes, and then I'm all yours."

"She yelled at me because he wouldn't look at the camera. Called me a crazy cat lady. And what's worse," he said, lowering his voice, "she called Felonious a fur ball." Henry whispered the last two words.

Caroline lowered her voice, hoping it would have a calming effect. "Please, if I can just get Mrs. Arnold and Alysha started, then we can switch off when Tiffany gets here."

Henry plowed on as if Caroline hadn't said a word. "I know that it might sound foolish to a person who doesn't have cats, but they have feelings, too. They don't like to be shouted at. You get that. Tiffany doesn't."

"I know, Henry," Caroline said. "I love your cats. But Mrs. Arnold has her daughter here, and Alysha needs to be somewhere soon." She wasn't going to tell Henry that Alysha was missing school today to have her portrait taken. The company that had done picture day at her elementary school had made no attempt to even capture Alysha looking straight ahead. Mrs. Arnold had e-mailed the pictures to Caroline, and she had been appalled. In one shot, Alysha's head had been tilted left and down, capturing a skewed profile of the girl. In another, she was looking up, slack-jawed with her eyes half closed.

"I'm not letting that cat Nazi anywhere near my girls. I don't care where that girl has to be," Henry said, motioning in the direction of Alysha. "No offense."

"No offense?" Mrs. Arnold said. "Do you think you can be rude to my daughter and then be forgiven by *no offense*?"

"I wasn't being rude to your daughter." Henry sounded legitimately surprised.

"No?" Mrs. Arnold said. "Then who?"

"I just want to keep my appointment."

"And you will," Caroline said

"It's fine," Mrs. Arnold said. "Let his cats go first."

"This isn't a cat versus human thing," Henry explained. "It's the principle. I had an appointment."

"So does Mrs. Arnold," Caroline said.

"But mine is with you. *Her* photographer is late," he said, pointing at Mrs. Arnold.

"There's such a thing as acting like a gentleman," Mrs. Arnold said.

"I take offense to that," Henry said. "Letting you go first would be sexist. Gender plays no role here. Ladies before gentlemen is completely patriarchal."

"I wasn't talking about me," Mrs. Arnold said. "I was talking about my daughter. She's the one having her photograph taken. I thought it would be nice for her to see a gentleman in action."

"She's a girl, too," Henry said, sounding petulant. "Still a gender issue."

"She's a child," Mrs. Arnold said.

"So you get to cut just because you have a kid?"

"Henry!" Caroline said. "Please."

"Oh, for goodness sake," Mrs. Arnold said to Caroline. "Please just take this man first. Me and Alysha will be fine."

"Alysha and I," Henry corrected.

"Excuse me?" Mrs. Arnold said, rising from her seat.

At that moment, Caroline's phone rang, stopping Henry before he could fire off his retort. She removed the phone from her pocket, apologizing for taking the call. She hoped it was Tiffany, calling to say that she was five minutes down the street. She looked down at the screen. It was Polly's school.

Caroline pressed the phone to her ear. "Hello?" She listened intently. "I understand," she said after a moment. "I'll be right there. Fifteen minutes."

"You're leaving?" Henry asked.

"I have to," Caroline said, stuffing the phone back into her pocket. "It's my daughter's school."

"You can't just leave," Henry said. "I have an appointment. You can't just walk out. And what about those two? They have an appointment, too."

"Now you're worried about our appointment?" Mrs. Arnold asked.

Caroline had to go. She had no choice. But she couldn't just run off without somehow getting Henry Parker and Mrs. Arnold to leave first. Henry was right. She couldn't just leave them here waiting.

"Please," she said. There was that word again. "It's an emergency. I need to get to my daughter's school now. Could you all just wait outside? Tiffany will be here any minute."

"Are you canceling our appointment?" Mrs. Arnold asked.

"And what about Georgio McGovern and Temptress?" Henry asked, lifting the pet carrier to give Caroline a glimpse of the cats. "I need them photographed today."

"Please," Caroline said. "It really is an emergency."

"I told you. I'm not letting Tiffany anywhere near my cats," Henry barked.

"Okay, Henry, let's take it down a notch or two and relax."

Heads turned to the front door. Even Georgio McGovern (or maybe it was Temptress) turned in the direction of the voice. It was Tiffany. She was standing just inside the doorway, her arms crossed, smiling. Caroline had the impression that she had been standing there awhile.

Tiffany was wearing a navy blue skirt, a matching jacket, and heels. Her dark hair was pinned up. Her makeup was subtle and immaculate. But her appearance was beside the point. She could've been wearing one of Polly's T-shirts and still exude authority.

"You're not shooting my cats!" Henry said.

"Henry, I'd love to shoot your cats," Tiffany said. "But there are laws about these things."

Mrs. Arnold laughed.

Even Henry chuckled a tiny bit, despite himself.

As if the laughter had opened a door, Tiffany stepped through it and joined the group. "Mrs. Arnold," she said. "My name is Tiffany. I'm a photographer here. Sorry I was late, but Caroline needs to go." Then she turned to Caroline and smiled. "Is that right?"

"Yes," she said. "Polly's school called. I have to go." She hated how answering to Tiffany's authority placed her in the same category as Henry Parker and Mrs. Arnold, but there it was. Typical Caroline.

"So here's what we're going to do," Tiffany said, directing her attention back to Henry. "I'm going to take care of Mrs. Arnold and Alysha's shoot first, because Alysha is missing school right now, and we don't want that. And we're not going to make Caroline feel guilty for leaving, because you know that if your cat needed you, you'd drop everything and run to him, too. Right?"

"But I had—"

"I know you're not happy, Henry, but that's okay. Emergencies aren't supposed to make people happy." She turned to Caroline and winked. "Caroline, you'll call and let us know that Polly's okay?"

"Sure, but I might be able to get Mrs. Arnold out of here in a couple minutes. Before I go."

Tiffany smiled. "You shot some B-roll?"

Caroline nodded. "Mrs. Arnold, can you and Alysha just follow me into the studio?"

"Don't you need to go?" Mrs. Arnold asked. "It's okay. I understand."

"I do. But this will only take a minute."

"What's B-roll?" Henry asked. "Do I get B-roll?"

Caroline ignored the question and led Mrs. Arnold, who was pushing Alysha's wheelchair, into the studio.

"This will sound strange," Caroline said once the door was closed. "But I was hiding in the bushes when you arrived. That's why I walked in after you."

"Hiding in the bushes?"

"Yes. So I could shoot you and your daughter. Sometimes it's hard for people to appear natural in a photo session. Especially kids like Alysha. Sometimes the best shots are taken when no one knows you're watching. I know it sounds weird, but I think I got a few that you might like. Can I show you?"

Mrs. Arnold nodded, but she looked unconvinced.

Caroline connected her camera to a computer. Photos that she had taken from behind the bushes appeared on a large screen above the keyboard. She scrolled through several wide angle shots before she came to the ones of just Mrs. Arnold and Alysha's faces. "Like this one, maybe?"

It was a picture of Alysha, looking up toward the sky at a slight angle. It was impossible to discern her position because only her face appeared in the frame, but Caroline had shot it while Alysha was in her mother's arms, being lowered into the wheelchair. The girl was beaming. Looking up at her mother with love and trust and maybe even a little joy. A mother and daughter in a private moment that likely occurred several times a day. Caroline had chosen her spot well. The angle of the sun had ignited a sparkle in Alysha's eyes and had alighted her cheeks in a yellow glow.

"Or this one?" Caroline said, scrolling to a nearly identical shot. She had been shooting fast, capturing several images a second, so there were many to choose from. "Or this? I have some of them with you, too," she said. "And I took some—"

Mrs. Arnold sniffled. Tears welled in her eyes. Alysha was looking at the screen, too. Staring at it. Her smile even larger now than it had been in the parking lot.

"Do you like them?" Caroline asked.

"No," Mrs. Arnold said. "I love them. They're beautiful."

"Your daughter's beautiful."

"Sometimes I think I'm the only one who sees it. But you see it, too. I can tell. I can see it in these pictures." She wiped her eyes with her sleeve. "I want these," she said, pointing at the screen. "All of them."

Caroline sat down at the computer and began working. In a minute, she had transferred all the images from her camera to a flash drive. She passed it over to Mrs. Arnold. "They're yours. Free of charge. If you want prints, we can do that, too. I'll have to charge you for them, but the images are yours. On the house."

"No," Mrs. Arnold said.

"Yes. It was an honor to shoot the two of you."

Mrs. Arnold reached out and hugged Caroline tightly. "Thank you," she said. "You have no idea what this means to me. And to Alysha." She turned to her daughter. "Alysha, do you like the pictures?" she asked, pointing to the one still on the screen.

Alysha smiled and said, "Yay."

"I'm so glad," Caroline said, smiling back at the girl. "Now I really need to go. I'm going to leave out the back, so I don't have to see Mr. Parker again. Okay?"

"Of course. He's a silly little man."

"I guess we're all a little silly at times. But I like Henry. Most days, at least."

"Good luck with your daughter."

"Thanks," Caroline said. She had a feeling she'd need all the luck she could get.

six

Benjamin Banneker High School reminded Caroline of her own high school. Long corridors with endless rows of narrow, dented lockers. Faded linoleum floors. Bulletin boards crowded with notices about basketball tryouts and marching band fund-raisers. Antibullying posters. The aroma of cheap carpeting, cheaper cologne, and the constant struggle against the onslaught of hormonal perspiration.

Students clustered in the hallways in small, distinct groups, rarely intermingling, aggressively unaware of those around them. Instead of the stacks of books that Caroline had carried when she was their age, these students held phones in their hands, their eyes rapidly shifting from faces to phone and back again. There were other things that Caroline didn't recall from her high school days. The intercom, camera, and buzzer at the front door. Security guards patrolling the hallways. Headphones and earbuds jammed into ears and dangling around necks. Water bottles. Tattoos and facial piercings. It was as if nothing had changed and everything had changed.

As she approached the office, Caroline couldn't help but feel as if she were in at least as much trouble as her daughter.

Polly was sitting on a wooden bench opposite the high counter that separated students and parents from the inner sanctum of the high school office. She turned as Caroline entered, her eyes wide and pleading, making her look younger than she had in a long time. She stared at her mother for several seconds—a lifetime in this world of cell phones, headphones, and teen angst—before slowly returning her gaze to her laceless, lime-green sneakers.

She looks so small, Caroline thought. Though Polly was short and slim, her personality had always made her seem larger. Louder. But at this moment, she looked almost tiny on that bench. Hunched and muted. Wounded, even.

Caroline did not like it.

"Can I help you?" one of the secretaries asked without rising from her swivel chair.

"Yes, I'm Caroline Jacobs. Polly's mother. Dr. Powers asked me to come in."

"Of course. Just one moment, Ms. Jacobs."

Ms. Jacobs. The secretaries had undoubtedly been trained to avoid all assumptions lest they offend anyone. Caroline felt she should correct the woman. Let her know that she was a *Mrs.* and kind of liked being one. But she let it go.

A moment later a door opened and a short, balding man stepped out. "Ms. Jacobs?" he asked, removing his glasses and nodding in her direction. "I'm Dr. Powers. Come in, please."

Caroline turned and looked back at Polly, still sitting quietly on the bench. Her gaze remained fixed on her sneakers.

"Polly can wait here a moment while we talk if that's all right," Dr. Powers said. He was smiling, encouraging her to step forward, and yet she knew that it was not a real smile. It was an administrative smile. One designed to produce action.

"Okay," Caroline said and followed him into his office.

The room had no windows. It was small, with barely enough space for a desk and a cluster of wooden chairs. It was poorly lit. The walls were bare. Dingy. Like a closet. Not what she had expected from a principal's office.

"Have a seat, Ms. Jacobs," Dr. Powers said, assuming a position on the opposite side of the desk. "Mrs. Thompson will be joining us as well. To take notes."

As if on cue, the woman from behind the counter entered the

office, taking a position in the far corner of the room. She had a legal pad in her hand. Once seated, she looked over Dr. Powers's shoulder at Caroline. Her expression was flat. Emotionless.

"Let's get started," Dr. Powers said. "Thank you for coming in so quickly."

"Did you call my husband?" Caroline asked.

"One of my secretaries left a message. Have we heard back?" he asked, glancing over his shoulder.

"No," Mrs. Thompson said, lifting her eyes from the legal pad and staring blankly at Caroline once again.

"Did you call your husband?" Dr. Powers asked.

"I did. I left a message, too."

Caroline tried to remember where Tom was supposed to be right now. A sales call for the replacement windows? Something for the church? She wasn't sure. "He's probably meeting with a client," she said. "Or maybe someone from the congregation."

"Congregation?"

"Yes. Tom's the deacon of the First Congregational Church. Over on Willowbrook."

"Oh," Dr. Powers said. "Then I expect that he'll find this especially upsetting."

Mrs. Thompson nodded with great solemnity.

"Especially upsetting?" Caroline repeated. "What happened?"

"Your daughter attacked another student in the biology lab this morning."

"She attacked someone?"

"Yes," Dr. Powers said. "A classmate. Mr. Shultz said that the girls were arguing about something in the back of the classroom and then Polly began shouting. Using profanity, from what I'm told. Before Mr. Shultz could reach them to intervene, Polly had punched Miss Dinali in the face. In the nose, to be exact."

"Miss *Dinali*?" Caroline asked.

"Yes. Grace Dinali," Dr. Powers said. "Polly doesn't deny punching Grace, but she won't tell me what caused the fight or talk about it in any way. She refuses to discuss it."

"What does the other girl say?" Caroline asked.

"I haven't been able to speak to her. Grace's mother brought her to the hospital before we had a chance to talk."

"She had to go to the hospital?"

"Our nurse thinks it's just a bruise, but Mrs. Dinali was worried that Grace's nose might be broken. She wanted to be safe." Dr. Powers cleared his throat. "Obviously this is a serious situation, but Polly has never been in any real trouble before, so that will be taken into account. And I heard about the unfortunate incident at the PTO meeting last night. Is there something going on outside of school that might explain this sudden change in behavior?"

Not this sudden change *in Polly's behavior*, Caroline noted. She had been called into the principal's office just as much as her daughter had. "No," she said. "No changes."

"I'd like to keep the police out of this situation if at all possible, but that may not be up to me. Mrs. Dinali may feel the need to involve them. If it's determined that Polly has been bullying Grace, I'll be forced to investigate the incident more thoroughly. State law comes into play. But I can't do anything if she won't talk to me."

Caroline stopped listening. The dingy office, the ancient furniture, the blank-eyed stare of Mrs. Thompson, the scribbling of her pen, and Dr. Powers's administrative smile had all faded into nonspecific white noise. That spark in her belly had reignited.

"Are you sure there's nothing I need to know about, Ms. Jacobs?" Dr. Powers asked, sounding even more concerned. "Something going on between you and the Dinali family? Something going on at home?"

Caroline didn't answer. She was thinking of the fifteen-year-old version of herself. Thinking about a girl named Emily Kaplan and a Saturday morning ride to Strawberries.

It was twenty-five years ago.

It was yesterday.

"Ms. Jacobs?" Dr. Powers said. "Is there anything at all that I should know about?"

Caroline's eyes met his. She finally had something to say. That spark was now a fire in her belly again. It was warm and bright. "It's *Mrs*. Jacobs," she said with more force than she intended. "I'm married. You called my husband. Remember?"

"Of course. I'm sorry. Mrs. Jacobs."

"Is there a place where I can speak to my daughter alone?"

Dr. Powers blinked.

Mrs. Thompson stopped scribbling.

"I think it's better if I speak to her first," Caroline said. "Privately."

Dr. Powers drummed his fingers silently on the desk and stared. This was not a part of his plan. Caroline had gone off-script, and he was deciding how to improvise. Finally he said, "You can use Mr. Hugh's office across the hall. It's the guidance office, but he's out meeting with college recruiters today. It should be empty."

Caroline rose from her chair.

"I want to help, Ms.—er, *Mrs*. Jacobs. There's no need for this to become any bigger than it already is."

"Then let me see my daughter."

Caroline told herself to remain calm. Find out what happened before deciding what to do next. Work with Polly as a team. Figure a way out of this mess together. No need to yell. No need to escalate things.

"What the hell were you thinking?" Polly shouted as soon as the door to the guidance office clicked shut. "You make jokes about the noble gases at breakfast but don't bother to mention that you told Grace Dinali's mother to fuck off?"

Polly had assumed an upright posture that Caroline had rarely seen, despite her constant urgings to straighten up. Her fists were clenched. She was breathing through her mouth. She looked ready to punch someone. Again.

"Hey, I'm not the one who just punched someone in the face," Caroline said. "What were you thinking?"

"I was thinking that I couldn't let Grace Dinali insult my mother without doing something about it. When I told her to shut up, she told me that I needed to shut my bitch mother up. So I punched her."

"Stop swearing," Caroline said.

"Why should I? You weren't worried about swearing last night."

"Just calm down. Okay?"

"Calm down?" Polly said, throwing her hands in the air. "Do you have any idea what you did? Grace Dinali didn't even know I existed yesterday. And that was *a good thing.* Now I'm her biggest enemy. She hates my guts. Do you have any idea what that means for me? Why didn't you tell me what you said last night?"

"I had no idea Mary Kate Dinali would run home and tell her daughter."

"Mom, everyone ran home and told their kids. *Everyone* knew about it this morning. Everyone except for me. You sent me into a freakin' ambush."

She was right, of course. Caroline had sent her daughter into the lion's den without as much as a warning. "Fine," she admitted. "You're right. I should've warned you. But that doesn't mean you get to punch a girl in the face."

"What if someone had called Grandma a bitch? What would you have done?"

Caroline said nothing. She knew exactly what she would've done. Or more precisely, what she would not have done. She was suddenly, almost overwhelmingly, flushed with pride and appreciation for her daughter. Envy, too. Polly had risen up and defended her mother's honor. Even though the two could barely carry on a conversation, Polly had punched a girl in the nose because she had insulted her mother. Punched a popular girl, too.

Just as quickly, her pride and appreciation was replaced with shame. Shame for placing her daughter in this position. Shame for what she had failed to do in her own life. Shame for all that had happened as a result of her inaction.

It was that moment, that very instant, that Caroline's idea was born. The boldest, craziest idea of her life. It wasn't a fully formulated plan. It wasn't even a fully formulated idea. But it was the beginning of an idea. The spark. More than that, it was a sudden, moral imperative that Caroline could not ignore. Caroline Jacobs knew that if she didn't act now, she never would.

"C'mon," she said, taking Polly's balled-up fist in her hand. "We're going."

"You realize Dr. Powers is going to totally suspend me. Right? He might even expel me."

"We're not going to see Dr. Powers."

"What do you mean?"

"We're leaving," Caroline said, tugging harder at her daughter's arm.

"Where are we going?" Caroline didn't answer, so Polly asked again. "Mom, where are we going?"

"Home."

seven

"Why are we getting on the highway?" Polly asked.

Caroline said nothing.

"*Mom?* Where are we going?"

Still nothing.

"Mom!"

"Don't shout. I'm right here."

"Then answer my question."

"I'm going home," Caroline said. "You're coming for the ride."

"What do you mean you're going home? This isn't the way home."

"Blackstone." Saying it aloud made the plan feel a little more real. "We're going to Blackstone."

"We're going to Grandma's house?" Polly asked. "Mom, Massachusetts is like nine hours away. Are you crazy?"

"Maybe. Yes. Probably. But we're going."

"What are you talking about?" Polly asked. "I have to go to school tomorrow. I have soccer practice."

"You're going to be suspended. You said it yourself."

"This is crazy," Polly said. "I'm not driving all the way to Massachusetts with you. Does Dad even know what you're doing?"

"I'll call him and fill him in."

"I'm calling him right now," Polly said, jamming her hand into her bag for her phone.

"No. Don't!" Caroline reached over to grab the phone from

Polly's hand and in the process sent the car careening into the adjacent lane. A pickup swerved to avoid them.

"Jesus, Mom!" Polly shouted. "You're going to kill us!"

"Just put the phone away. I don't want you calling Dad right now."

"Why not?"

Caroline considered for a moment and opted for honesty. "If I call him now, he'll talk me out of going. We need to get far enough away that there's no turning back."

"What are you talking about?"

"I just want to drive. Okay? I just want to get out of Maryland and get through Delaware. Then we can call him. Put whatever you want on the radio. Stick your earbuds in. I don't care. Just let me get some distance between us and home."

"Are you leaving him? Are you guys getting a divorce or something?" Polly suddenly sounded worried. Hysterical, even. "Is that why you freaked out last night?"

"No, this isn't about me and your father at all. We're fine. I just need to do something he wouldn't like."

"I don't want to go to Grandma's house," Polly said. "Even if I'm going to be suspended, I still have a life. I can't just drive to Massachusetts in the middle of the week. Can't you please just drop me off at home first?"

"No," Caroline said. "I want you with me."

"I don't care what you want. I don't want to go."

Polly was twisting the cords on her sweatshirt. It was something she did when she was nervous, something she had been doing since she was a little girl. She would twist shoelaces, napkins, sleeves, elastics, paper, and even her hair if she was nervous enough.

"You don't have a choice," Caroline said, more sternly than she had intended. "I want you with me."

"This is ridiculous. Why am I here?"

Caroline stared at the road ahead. The interstate stretched to a pale blue horizon. Many horizons between them and their destination. Just let me get a few of them between us and home, she thought, and I'll be okay.

"Mom, you can't just ignore me. I'll start screaming if I have to. I'll scream my head off right in this car. This isn't fair. You can't just drag me to Massachusetts because you feel like it!"

"Listen," Caroline finally said. "I'll explain everything to you. I promise. But can you just give me a little while to think? Let's just drive for a while. Okay?"

"I want to go home."

"I need you to trust me. And I need you to come with me. Please."

Polly said nothing for what felt like a long time. Caroline knew that her daughter was waiting for her to crack. She knew how uncomfortable her mother was with silence. But this time, Caroline vowed to remain quiet until Polly spoke.

"Fine," Polly finally said. "Whatever. But this is crazy. You're crazy. First the PTO meeting and now this. You need some serious help, Mom." She reached into her bag again and removed her phone.

"And no phones," Caroline said. "Okay?"

"I just want to text Peyton. Tell her that my mother Patty Hearsted me."

"Patty Hearsted you?"

"Geez, Mom. Patty Hearst? Stockholm syndrome? Are you sure you went to college?"

"Can you just put the phone away?" Caroline said. "Let this be just you and me for a while?"

As if in protest, Caroline's phone rang. Polly picked it up off the console and looked at the display. "It's the school. Dr. Powers is probably pissed that you broke me out."

"Don't answer it. I just want to drive for a while. No phones. No texts. Just us. Okay?"

There was another protracted silence before Polly spoke again. "Fine, but you're scaring me. And pissing me off, too."

Taking Polly out of school had made sense to Caroline. Freeing her from the clutches of Dr. Powers and his pasty-faced secretary seemed like the only thing she could do. There was no way that she was going to lead her daughter into that dingy little office and give the principal the opportunity to suspend her after she had defended her mother's honor.

But there was more to it than that. The truth was . . . well, Caroline didn't know what the truth was. She suspected it was a combination of several things, chief among them her desire not to be alone. Had she been heading north on her own, she probably would've turned back already. Somehow, despite Polly's protests, her presence had emboldened her. Made her feel braver than she had felt in a long time.

And she was going to need it. Caroline may have found the courage to stand up to Mary Kate Dinali. She may have had the audacity to remove her daughter from school. But returning to Blackstone and executing her plan would require a lot more courage—the kind of courage possessed by a girl who could punch a popular girl in the nose.

Mother and daughter didn't say a word for almost an hour, but the silence was welcome, at least for Caroline. It gave her a chance to decide how much of the story she would tell Polly—and how much she would not.

"I'm sorry I didn't tell you about the PTO meeting," Caroline finally said, breaking the silence. They were on the New Jersey Turnpike. The sun was low on the horizon, and clouds were building in the west. "I didn't realize that it would affect you. But I should have."

"No kidding."

"I can't undo it," Caroline said. "But I really feel bad about it."

"Is it true you told Grace's mom to fuck off?"

"I really wish you wouldn't swear."

"Mom, if you're going to kidnap me, drive me a million miles from home without letting me pack a toothbrush or a change of underwear, you could at least be straight with me. Besides, I'm only quoting you. Right?"

"I said some things last night that I shouldn't have," Caroline admitted.

"I can't believe it. You're like a houseplant in those meetings."

"A houseplant is stretching it a bit."

"Yeah, right. Remember last year when you made me ask the questions about the Cape Cod tournament?"

"I know," Caroline said. "Lay off."

"I mean, you never talk in any meetings."

"*I know,*" she repeated. "I get it."

"Then why'd you do it?" Polly asked "What did Grace's mom say that turned you into a crazy person?"

"Nothing, really. At least nothing that she hasn't said before. She was telling us how we weren't doing enough for the school. How the same people were stepping up again and again for every event."

"That's it?"

"Yeah, I know," Caroline said. "But then she went after this woman who didn't deserve it. A woman trying to do the best she can. I just lost it."

"Mom, you've never lost it in your entire life. You're like the total opposite of losing it."

"I know."

"So what happened?"

Caroline sighed. "I don't know."

"C'mon. It must have been something. You don't just flip your lid for nothing."

"I just got upset. Okay?"

"Right," Polly said, anger returning to her voice.

"What?"

Polly said nothing. She stared ahead. Folded her arms.

"What?" Caroline said, anger in her own voice now.

"The least you could do is tell me the truth."

"I'm serious," Caroline said. "I just got upset."

"Mom, someone could be chopping your hands and feet off with a butter knife and you still wouldn't complain. I've never seen you lose your temper once. Not even with me, and I deserve it. *A lot*. I love you, but you get walked all over all the time and never say a word. You expect me to believe that some lady who acts like a bitch all the time acted like a bitch again and you lost your mind?"

Polly was right. She deserved to know. Not all of it, of course, but the beginning at least. "Fine. I'll tell you. You have the right to know." She thought for a moment, wondering where to begin. Where do you start the story of your life? "I was picked on when I was your age."

"Big surprise."

"What do you mean?"

"I saw your yearbook," Polly said. "You weren't exactly cool."

"Yeah. Well, I wasn't. But I wasn't hopeless, either. You know what I mean?"

"Not really."

"You know how there are kids who never quite fit in? They're awkward or overweight or they stutter or something like that?

"Yeah?"

"I wasn't a weird one," Caroline said. "I just wasn't cool enough. I was shy. I was *so shy*. I still am. And I didn't have the right clothes or the right shoes. And I didn't have a lot of friends. And your grandmother didn't help the situation."

"After Grandpa left?"

"Yeah. Your grandmother was a mess for a long time. I guess I was, too."

"And Aunt Lucy? Was this before she—"

"Around the same time. And Mom just wasn't there for me."

"All that sucks," Polly said. "But what does this have to do with last night?"

"I think that when Mary Kate was talking to us like that, I felt like she was talking to me. It was like I was getting picked on all over again. And we were sitting in a high school cafeteria, so I think that may have escalated it. You know? Kind of like a perfect storm."

"What did the high school cafeteria have to do with it?"

"I guess everything sort of started going downhill for me in the high school cafeteria. It's where things went bad first. Turned me into a real outsider. And sort of turned me inside myself, too."

"What happened?" Polly asked.

Caroline took a deep breath. "I've never told anyone this before."

"Maybe you were waiting to tell me."

Caroline laughed. "Maybe." She'd held this secret in so long that it felt like a part of her. As critical to survival as her heart or lungs.

"So?" Polly said. "It's not like you're letting me talk to anyone else. And no time like the present. Right?"

"I guess."

"Keeping secrets is actually bad for you," Polly said. "It stresses your frontal cortex. Sticks a roadblock in your brain that keeps you from moving onto other things."

"Seriously?"

"You doubt me?" Polly asked.

"Did you learn that in school?"

"No," Polly said. "I read it in *Forbes*."

"Seriously?"

"Seriously. Now c'mon. I want to hear."

"I can't believe I'm doing this."

"Just shut up and talk."

"Fine," Caroline said. She felt like she was standing on the edge of a cliff, about to plunge into a sea of freezing water. Once she began, there would be no turning back. "Her name was Emily Kaplan. We were best friends. At least I thought we were."

"What happened?"

Caroline smiled. "Nothing good. After it happened, I tried

to never think about it again. But I guess I never stopped thinking about it."

"What happened?"

Caroline decided to tell Polly the story. Not the whole story, but the first half.

The part before she killed Lucy.

eight

Caroline had been naïve. Everything she knew about high school had come from movies like *The Breakfast Club* and *Fast Times at Ridgemont High*. She expected a campus rather than a school, with large swaths of unsupervised space and enormous blocks of un-scheduled time. She expected well-lit hallways lined with lockers and trophy cases, a gleaming cafeteria, a football field, and a col-lection of odd and easy-to-fool teachers.

And she expected the students to be divided into clearly delin-eated categories. Caroline didn't really think she'd fit into any of the cliques. She wasn't a jock or a cool kid, a stoner or an outcast. But she hoped to achieve a sort of Molly Ringwald–type status. She would be the girl who was a little shy and a little poor, who would eventually find her tribe and earn the grudging respect of the masses.

That was the problem with being naïve. You went into things entirely unprepared.

Caroline didn't get her Brat Pack utopia. At Blackstone-Millville Regional High School she found low-hanging ceilings, dim, fluo-rescent lighting, and a dingy cafeteria that smelled of spoiled milk. Worse, she was faced with a highly structured, well-supervised environment with four minutes between classes, a complete ab-sence of free time, and a draconian emphasis on homework. There was no football team. No quirky teachers. There were cliques, all right, but most kids didn't fit into those convenient boxes. Some dumb jocks were smart. Some cool kids were mean. There were popular stoners, articulate stoners, sad stoners, and everything in between. Whole categories Caroline hadn't even thought about. Punks. Princesses. Good-looking geeks. The aggressively college bound. The clinically depressed. The invisible kids. So many invisible kids.

Standing on that sidewalk on the first day of school, Caroline was filled with misconceptions. She was frightened, but she was hopeful. Foolishly hopeful.

Emily Kaplan's idea of high school had been entirely different. Pretty, intelligent, and charming, bolstered by the wealth of her yuppie parents and her only-child status, Emily was a confident kid well armed for high school. Confident people, Caroline thought, didn't worry. They did not plan. They possessed an expectation that they could overcome any challenge placed before them. It's not that the world bent entirely to Emily's needs—even she had her disappointments—it's that she carried herself with the confidence of a person who believed it eventually would. Emily was nervous on the first day of high school, but ultimately, she knew that she would find her way and come out on top. Because she always had.

"The John F. Kennedy of children." That's how Caroline's mother had referred to Emily. Caroline hadn't understood the reference at the time, but even if she had, it wouldn't have mattered. Emily's social skills were of little consequence to Caroline. For Caroline, it was much simpler. Emily was her best friend. The person who knew her best. The person who made her the happiest. Their friendship was a miracle of sorts. Caroline's luckiest break.

"Did you actually like Emily?" Polly asked.

"I loved Emily. You couldn't not love her. And as little kids, we were together all the time. I spent more time with Emily than anyone else. That history meant something."

The two girls had grown up across the street from each other. Up until eighth grade, Caroline and Emily had spent at least a portion of every day together. And when they weren't in school, they were often together for the entire day.

In childhood, proximity matters. It matters a lot.

"And I knew that being friends with Emily was good for me," Caroline explained. "I knew it made me . . . not exactly popular, but less invisible."

"So you were a name dropper?" Polly asked, a smirk spreading across her face.

"Maybe," Caroline admitted. "When stuff like that started to matter. But when we were little, we were more like sisters."

"What about Aunt Lucy?" Polly asked. "Where was she?"

"Lucy was four years younger than me, which is like a million years younger when you're a kid. I was in second grade before Lucy could even walk. Emily and I would let her hang out with us sometimes, but mostly we left her at home. There was a little girl who lived two houses over. Patty something, I think. Lucy spent a lot of time with her."

"So you bagged on your sister?" Polly said.

"No," Caroline said, not entirely sure what *bagging on her sister* meant. "Lucy and I were close. We would sit on the couch under the same blanket at night and watch TV and eat popcorn. And Lucy would climb into my bed whenever she had a nightmare, which was like every night. But I couldn't talk to her like I could to Emily. She was just too young."

Caroline's father had built a tree house for her when she was in kindergarten. It had been a safe haven for Caroline and Emily throughout most of their school years. Built within the bifurcated trunk of a towering oak at the edge of the tree line, it represented a demarcation of sorts for them. On one side stood Caroline's backyard. Civilization, where a glass of water or a Band-Aid could be had in a moment's notice. On the other side stood the untamed copse that filled the swath of land between Farm and Lincoln Streets, an area that Caroline and Emily had called the Deep Dark Wood.

Until they were old enough to care about skinned knees, muddy socks, and mosquito bites (and that came later for them than most girls), this was where Caroline and Emily had spent most of their childhood. They caught frogs in the trickle of water that they called Bloody River because it was where Emily had once gashed her elbow on a rock. They swung on the teenagers' rope swing over Getchell's Pond, perfecting their Tarzan calls and clinging on for dear life. They read novels by Judy Blume and Lois Lowry beneath a low-hanging pine tree and argued over which one of them most resembled Margaret and Claire. They hiked and climbed and crawled and swam like only free-range children of a generation ago could.

But no matter how long they spent exploring the forest, they would eventually find their way back to the tree house and to their favorite positions on either side of the small, rectangular room. There they would talk for hours, feasting on Flaky Puffs and Junior Mints and drinking cans of warm Mello Yello.

Caroline had never been more true to herself than in those early days with Emily. Competition and envy didn't exist between the girls. Their friendship had no room for ego or deceit. That was simply the way it was. And it was perfect.

Caroline's father left on Saint Patrick's Day when she was seven years old. He went out to the Firehouse Pub and never came home. At the time, Caroline didn't entirely understand what had happened. Her father drove a truck and was often gone for two or three weeks at a time. She assumed that he was on another road trip. The two had been close when she was little, but the cross-country trips, combined with what Caroline later understood to be her father's descent into alcoholism and depression, had driven them apart. She loved her father, but she stopped needing him because he wasn't around to be needed.

Proximity, it turns out, works both ways.

Caroline came home one day to find her mother crying at the dining room table. One of her father's bottles was on the table beside her, empty. "Your father left," she had said. "He doesn't want to come back. He's in Florida, and he wants to stay there."

"Do we have to move to Florida?" Caroline asked.

"No, hon. We don't."

"Okay. Good."

"You understand what I'm saying," her mother said, looking at her closely. "Right? Dad isn't coming home like he usually does."

"I know," Caroline said. But she didn't. Not really. "He'll be back for Easter, probably. And my birthday. And those aren't far away. It's just like a long trip in his truck. But he'll be back soon."

"Did he come back for your birthday?" Polly asked.

"No."

"Bastard," Polly said quietly.

Caroline was accustomed to her daughter's indignation, but it was usually directed at her. This was different. It was nice.

"My mother let things sink in slowly for me. Let me figure it out myself over time. I know it sounds rotten of me. I had just lost my dad, but I wasn't all that upset at first."

Polly screwed up her face. "Really?"

"Here's the thing . . . I was used to home being just Mom and Lucy and me. 'Just us girls,' as my mother would say when Dad was away, which was all the time. And I was in middle school. Getting ready for high school. I had so much to think about already. So much of my life to deal with. And back then, parents just weren't as enmeshed in their kids' lives like they are today. There were days when I would leave the house in the morning and not come home until the streetlights came on. And I still had Emily. Even more than my mother or Lucy, I had Emily. There's a time in your life, you know, when your parents and your family just aren't as important as your friends. At least that's the way it was for me."

"I get it," Polly said. Caroline knew that she did.

"Don't get me wrong," Caroline said. "My father broke my heart. It just took time. It broke a little bit at a time."

"He broke Grandma's heart, too," Polly said, more a statement than a question.

"Yes, but he broke hers all at once. Maybe that's why she was a disaster for so long. Then Mom was forced to sell the house, and we moved into the apartment on Main Street. That's when I really got angry at my father. I hate to say it, but it wasn't until we lost the house that I was really upset about him leaving."

"When your dad leaves you like that, you get to feel however the hell you want."

"Maybe so," Caroline said.

"There's no maybe about it, Mom," Polly said.

Caroline and Emily spent their last day in the tree house eating Junior Mints, listening to *The Karate Kid* soundtrack, and crying. Emily helped Caroline pack her bedroom into cardboard boxes, taking time to examine mementos that had accumulated over the years. Friendship bracelets. A mini-golf scorecard from a night at Weirs Beach. Notes about bitchy girls and annoying teachers passed across middle school classrooms. A ticket stub from their first concert. Memories piled neatly atop each other like an endless wall of Lincoln Logs. Caroline felt closer to Emily in that final day than she had ever felt before.

Then that perfect wall began to crumble. All her walls started coming down. With the loss of her father also went all of the family's discretionary income. Her mother began harping on lights left on and showers taking too long. They ate a lot of macaroni. Sometimes they had cereal for dinner. Then Caroline and Lucy were added to the free lunch roll at school.

The losses began piling up, one after another. Summer camp was canceled. Their membership to the Tupperware Pool Club was not renewed. Places that had been an integral part of Caroline's childhood were suddenly inaccessible and off-limits. It was like vast swaths of Caroline's childhood landscape had been annexed by some foreign power. The loss of her father and even the house had been quick, but it was these small losses that did the most damage. Death by a thousand humiliating cuts. The donations of food from the local church. The hand-me-downs that found their way into her dresser drawers. The end of family vacations. The kind words and generous offers from family and friends made unkind by their acknowledgment of the family's descent into poverty. Caroline quickly learned that the last thing a poor kid wants is for people to know that she is poor. Hunger is often preferable to charity.

Caroline's access to Emily seemed to have expired, too. The girls still spoke in school and saw each other after the final bell, but Caroline sensed the friendship slipping once the gravitational pull had been eliminated.

"I know it sounds crazy," Caroline said. "But just the fact that we started taking different buses made it hard," she said. "We went from a forty-five-minute bus ride every day to a quick good-bye at our lockers. This was before cell phones, so it wasn't like we could stay in constant contact like you and your friends do. I would go over to her house sometimes, but it was hard. I'd stare across the street at a house that used to be mine."

"First your dad and then Emily," Polly said.

"Yeah, I guess so," Caroline said. "I never thought about it like that, but yes. And you know, just like I didn't care about losing my father at first, I felt like Emily didn't care about losing me. I kept trying, but I never felt like she was trying back. She didn't always return my phone calls. Even though she could've taken me to the swim club as a guest as much as she wanted, she didn't invite me. She'd tell me she wasn't going, but when I'd call her house, her mother would tell me that she left for the club hours ago. She started dating this boy named Brian but didn't tell me for three days, which is like three centuries to a teenager. At least back then it was. And when she dumped him two weeks later, she never bothered to tell me that, either. That summer before high school was awful. I felt like everything was falling apart."

But then came the first day of high school. Thrown into an unknown and confusing world, Emily and Caroline stuck together, partly because they arrived in their new environment aboard the same bus once again, and partly because there is safety in numbers. Mostly it was because Emily and Caroline shared five classes together. They couldn't escape each other if they had tried.

Proximity was working its magic once again.

For a while, the girls were as close as they had ever been. They navigated the embarrassment of the girls' locker room together and learned to avoid the make-out corner of the library. And during that nerve-wracking first-week jostle for tables and seats in the cafeteria, Emily and Caroline had found an empty table where they were joined by four other similarly nervous girls.

Caroline was doing okay. She and Emily were doing okay together.

But by the time the Freshman-Senior Get Acquainted Dance rolled around in October, Emily had joined the cheerleading team and was dating Danny Pollock, a boy who'd been chasing her since seventh grade. The time that she and Emily had spent on the phone each night, talking about homework and boys, was now all but gone.

Meanwhile, Caroline's mother fell behind in rent. The family car was repossessed.

Then Ellie Randoph arrived.

It was early November when Ellie came to Blackstone High with a confidence usually reserved for star athletes and prom queens, despite the fact that she looked like no one else at school. With her fishnet stockings, black leather boots, and a seemingly endless supply of concert T-shirts, safety pins, and lace accessories, Ellie looked like she had stepped right out of a music video, which, for a small town of five thousand people who had yet to see MTV, was unusual to say the least. The older girls didn't like the way Ellie acted like she owned the school. But Ellie didn't care. She flirted with the boys and ignored the dirty looks, which turned out to be an effective strategy. By her third day at school she was working as a member of the theater club's design crew. By the end of her first week, she was walking with Emily to at least half her classes, muscling Caroline out of her usual spot on Emily's left side.

It was during one of these elbowing sessions that Caroline discovered Ellie's parents had bought Caroline's old home and that Ellie was now sleeping in her old bedroom.

"It killed me," Caroline said. "The thought that some other girl, exactly my age, was living in my house, in my room, was awful. The fact that it was Ellie Randolph made it a thousand times worse. I felt like I had been replaced. Perfectly replaced. No. Not even replaced. I felt like Ellie was an upgrade. An upgraded version of me."

"I would've been mad, too. Bitch stole your house, then she stole your friend," Polly said.

"Exactly," Caroline said, feeling relief in her daughter's validation even decades later. "The two of them started going to the Lincoln Mall all the time. I wanted to go, but Mom was working two jobs. She was never home, and you can only bum rides for so long. So we'd be walking down the hall, the three of us, and Emily and I would be talking about something that happened in class, then Ellie would mention something that happened in the arcade on Saturday and bam! End of conversation for me. She did that all the time. Even if I tried to join in Ellie would say things like, 'Sorry, but you really had to be there.' Even their names were practically the same. It was awful."

"So Emily turned out to be a dumb ass?" Polly asked.

"What do you mean?"

"Sounds like she let this new girl control her."

"I never thought of it like that," Caroline said. "I don't know . . . I think it was just nice for her to have someone who didn't have to be carried along all the time. Someone on her level. It was a terrible way to treat me, but I understood it. Even back then I understood it."

"There comes a point when a person is too understanding, Mom," Polly said. "You don't need to try to understand why someone is treating you like dirt. You can just hate them for it."

Caroline shook her head slightly and smiled. "I don't get it. You still don't know how to do a load of laundry, and you answer most of my questions by rolling your eyes, and I can't remember the last time I heard you say please, but then you say something like that, and it makes me think you're all grown up. That you understand things maybe even better than me."

"I know how to do laundry," Polly said. "I just hate doing it."

Caroline smiled again. Twice now in less than a minute. It broke her heart to think how rarely she smiled in the presence of her little girl these days. Somewhere between the sunny days of kindergarten, filled with crayon drawings of their home and trees and hand-flapping stories about her classmates and her teacher and these sullen, silent days of high school, she and Polly had diverged. A wedge had been positioned between the two, and it had been applying outward pressure ever since. Where had that happened? And why had she allowed it to continue for so long? Why had it taken something like this to bring them together again?

"So what happened?" Polly said. "That can't be the end of it."

"No. It was little things at first. I'd be walking toward them in the hall, and they'd start looking at me and whispering. The kind of whispering that you know is about you, but you'd seem like a crazy person if you accused them of it. You know what I mean?"

Polly nodded.

"Then they started passing notes. We all passed notes back then, but they weren't private like a letter or e-mail would be today. They were more like group texts on paper. Sometimes we'd have three or four girls adding to the note in a long chain. But Emily and Ellie started writing their notes on paper from this pink notebook. They told me that the pink notes were top secret. For their eyes only. Then they started adding girls to the top-secret list. Girls who we ate lunch with. Sat with in class. They called it the Top Secret Sisters. I kept waiting for them to add my name to the list, but they didn't. That hurt. And even worse, it became awkward. I'd be sitting in French class with Emily and a couple other girls, and they'd be passing these notes right in front of me. Right over me. Laughing about what was written. And I'd just be sitting there like an idiot. Trying not to make eye contact. Trying to act like I didn't care."

"Makes me want to punch every single one of them in the face right now," Polly said, and Caroline loved her for it.

"I know it sounds bad, but I knew that I wasn't the easiest friend to have, either. Mom's car was repossessed. I was living in a run-down apartment. I didn't have any money to do anything. I was stuck at home, babysitting Lucy all the time. I wasn't exactly the happiest person in the world."

"She was your friend," Polly snapped. Maybe the same way she snapped just before she punched Grace Dinali in the nose. "She should've treated you better. Especially then. When you needed her the most."

"It wasn't like she just dropped me the second Ellie arrived. Ellie wasn't in many of our classes, so a lot of the time it was still just Emily and me. And Emily came over to the apartment a couple times just to check on my mom. Make sure she was okay. It was sweet. But still, I knew that she was slipping away. And I knew that Ellie was a big reason for it."

"Gimme a break, Mom. It wasn't Ellie's fault. The girl sounds like a total bitch, but Emily was supposed to be your friend."

"I know. It's hard, because at first I thought that we were just drifting apart. It happens."

"This was not drifting apart. Those girls were bullies."

"It's not like they—"

"Mom, she was the definition of a bully. Exclusion. Isolation. Behind-the-back bullshit. I should know. My generation is the expert on bullying. It's all we ever hear about."

"It's all you ever hear about?"

"Are you kidding me?" Polly said. "Police officers started visiting our class in first grade to talk about it. And every grade after that. Stop, walk, and talk. Tattling versus reporting. What you're supposed to do as bystanders. We role play. We practice strategies. We have assemblies where weirdos in costumes sing and dance about bullying. I've been taught more about bullying than I have about the Civil War. I'm probably the only kid in my grade who knows what Pickett's Charge or the Appomattox Court House were. And I know you don't know what they were, either, but just trust me. Emily was a bully. Ellie, too."

"Things were different when I was your age. Bullying wasn't the thing it is today."

"Jesus Christ, Mom. A rose by any other name and all that bullshit. Chilean sea bass is really Patagonian toothfish, but the name doesn't change the way it tastes. You didn't call them bullies back then, but that's what they were. Fucking cowards who ganged up on you and made your life miserable."

Caroline didn't know why she continued to defend Emily, but she did. Old habits, maybe. "I always thought that Emily and Ellie had more in common than me and Emily, so it made sense that they would gravitate toward each other."

"Sure," Polly said, sounding exasperated now. "But they didn't have to be dicks about it. You can have more than one friend. You can make new friends without cutting out your oldest friend completely."

"A lot of the stuff that Emily and Ellie got into was stuff that I didn't even understand," Caroline said. "They were listening to bands like Black Flag and Suicidal Tendencies. Echo & the Bunnymen. The Meatmen. Music was so important. Liking the right music, but just knowing the music was even more important. It changed the way they dressed. The way they talked. God, I can't believe I remember all this. It must sound so pathetic . . ."

"It's not pathetic," Polly said, softening her voice a bit. "Of course you remember that stuff. It was high school. You remember stuff when you are younger because there are so many firsts. Lots of memorable moments. When you get old, it's same old, same old. Less new stuff to remember. It's why time seems to fly the older you get. Life isn't as interesting anymore."

"Is that really a thing?" Caroline asked.

"Seriously? Do you even read anymore?"

"It makes sense. I remember so much from that time. Emily and Ellie would watch *Saturday Night Live* every week and spent all day Monday talking about the skits and the monologue. It's all I would ever hear on Mondays."

"You had *Saturday Night Live* back then?"

Turned out Polly didn't know everything. "Yes, but I never got to watch it. Grandma wouldn't let me stay up that late. And there was no Internet back then, so it wasn't like I could catch up on YouTube the next day. Even if I wanted to listen to their music, it meant I'd have to find the tapes and buy them. I couldn't just use Google and know everything I needed to know to sound cool. It may be hard to believe—today's world is so different—but information cost money back then, and I had no money."

"You guys were living in the stone age," Polly said.

"It wasn't that long ago," Caroline said. "But the world really was different back then. I remember spending hours sitting in front of my mother's radio with a clunky plastic cassette recorder in my hand, just waiting to record a Meatmen or Black Flag song. And of course I never did. Emily and Ellie loved the most obscure bands. The ones that only college radio stations were playing. It sounds crazy, but I thought that if I could just find a way to listen to the same music, then I could talk to them about it. I could be cool."

Then came the day that changed everything.

It had started off well. An A on her French test. A smile from Randy Marcotte in English class. A substitute in gym who let the class hang out on the bleachers and do homework. Caroline was feeling good when she passed through the double doors into the already crowded cafeteria. She arrived late on Fridays—she had to walk across campus from typing class—so many of the students were already seated and eating by the time she got there.

As Caroline approached the lunch table, she saw that all six seats were occupied. She stopped, thinking for a moment that one of the orange discs had somehow broken off, leaving the table one seat short. Then she spotted Ellie. She and Emily were sitting side by side and laughing about something in one of Emily's notebooks. Ellie was wearing a Dead Kennedys T-shirt. Different than the one Emily was wearing, but the same band. As she drew closer, she heard Emily say something about someone named Simon Le Bon. "He's got such a stupid name, but he's wicked cute."

Caroline burned.

She approached the table. Heads turned. No one made eye contact. Not Kimberly, who Caroline knew from homeroom. Not Janet, who sat next to her in history. Not even Molly, who Caroline helped with algebra almost every day. They weren't exactly looking away from her, but they weren't looking at her, either. It was as if they were looking right through her. As if she was nothing. Invisible.

"Hi, Ellie," Caroline said. "I think you're in my seat."

Ellie smiled. It was the smile of someone who knew she had already won. A king-of-the-mountain smile. A fuck-you smile. "I am?" she said. "I didn't know. Emily invited me to sit with her today."

Caroline looked to Emily.

"I wish we could just pull up a chair," Emily said. "But we're stuck with these stupid stools."

"Yeah, but that's my seat," Caroline said. "You can't just give away my seat."

"It's not like they're assigned," Emily said. "This isn't middle school."

Someone giggled.

"Yeah, but I've been sitting there since the first day of school. No offense, Ellie, but that's my seat."

Caroline knew she was fighting a losing battle. She had been ousted, at least for the day, though deep down, she knew that she had been permanently banished.

"Don't be ridiculous," Emily said. "Ellie can sit wherever she wants. And I want to sit with her today."

Ellie smiled again. "Emily went to the mall yesterday, and she's been dying to tell me about all the stuff she bought, so I thought we could talk during lunch. We only have chemistry and home-room together."

"And it's not stuff you'd be interested in," Emily added.

Caroline stuttered. She wanted to say something clever. Some-thing that might diffuse the situation. Make her sound cool. Casual. No big deal. Preserve some dignity for another day. But with six pairs of eyes affixed to her, not to mention the gaze of people at nearby tables now drawn to the possibility of conflict, all Caroline managed to say was "Why—"

"Why?" Emily said, filling the gap between words. "You need a reason why I want to sit with Ellie? How about she's my friend? Isn't that good enough?"

"But you're *my* friend," Caroline said. And instantly regret-ted it.

Emily rolled her eyes. "I'm not saying I don't want to be your friend. I just need some room for new friends. Ellie and I have stuff in common that you and I don't. We're not little girls any-more."

"Emily!" Ellie said. "Don't be mean. I'm sure you still have a few things in common. Right, Caroline?"

More giggles.

"I was just thinking maybe I could pull up a chair so we could all fit," Caroline managed.

"Jesus Christ, Caroline, we don't need to be attached twenty-four-seven. Could I just get a break? Just once?"

And just like that, Caroline was on her own.

"Emily?" Caroline said. Pleaded.

"What?"

"Is this for real?"

"I just need a break," Emily said, her voice softening. "Okay? We've been stuck at the hip for such a long time. I just want a break."

"Fine," Caroline said, her anger rising again. In that moment, an image of her father entered her mind. He had wanted a break, too. "Fine," she repeated, feeling the first tears form in her eyes. "But I want my seat back. I'm serious. You can't just kick me out like this."

Caroline braced for the counterattack that never came. Emily rose from her stool first, followed Ellie. Then Kimberly and Molly, and a few seconds later, Janet and Briana. "Fine," Emily said, and without another word, all six girls walked past Caroline toward the other side of the cafeteria.

"Wait," Caroline said. "You don't have to go."

The suddenly empty table might as well have been an erupting volcano. It drew the attention of almost every eye in the cafeteria.

Caroline was alone. Her seat was empty. The whole table was empty.

"Shit, Mom," Polly said. "That was harsh. Talk about mean girls."

"I know it was a long time ago. I know it sounds adolescent and silly, but I sometimes think that if it weren't for those stools, then things would've turned out different," Caroline said. "One more stool and everything that happened afterward would've been different."

"I don't know, Mom. It sounds like Emily was done with you, seat or no seat."

nine

By the time Caroline had finished her story, she and Polly were sitting in a diner somewhere in northern Jersey, a basket of fries and two Cokes occupying the table between them. It was raining now. The large windows of the diner were streaked with thin rivulets of water. Polly and Caroline were still drying off from the sprint from the car to the diner. Polly's hair was wet and flat. Her T-shirt hung limp from her shoulders. It was strange for Caroline to see her daughter look so disheveled. So natural. Like a little girl again. Gone was the carefully constructed image in which she emerged from her bedroom each day, the armor she wore to face the world.

Caroline couldn't believe that she had just told that story for the first time in her life, and to her teenage daughter no less.

"So what'd you do?" Polly asked, leaning forward as if there was more to the story.

"What do you mean?" Caroline asked between bites.

"What'd you do after Emily dissed you?"

"I didn't do anything," Caroline said. "I went to the library. I skipped lunch. End of story."

"No, I mean what did you eventually do?"

Caroline jammed a handful of fries into her mouth. She needed a moment to think. She had acted. Soon after, in fact. But she had already promised herself that the story, at least for Polly, would end there.

"I didn't do anything," Caroline finally said. "I didn't go back to the cafeteria all year."

"Are you kidding me? You didn't eat lunch for the rest of the year? How is that even possible?"

"I spent my lunch period in the library, okay? I tried to bring in sandwiches when I could, but—"

"But you were a free lunch kid."

"Yeah, I was. Grandma was having a hard enough time keeping food on the table without me taking it to school."

"So you didn't eat lunch for the rest of the year?" Polly shook her head slightly, almost imperceptibly. And then—perhaps taking a cue from Caroline—she stuffed a handful of fries into her mouth before shifting her gaze to the rain-streaked window and the parking lot beyond.

Polly may have understood the gravity of the incident. But she didn't know what the incident had set in motion. She could never know.

So many things could be traced back to that moment in the cafeteria. That's what Caroline had always thought. And yet she had also wondered if she hadn't blown the whole thing out of proportion—made an overly dramatic reaction to the kind of mundane cruelty that happens every day. She had often wondered if the course of her life had been determined not by the malice of a childhood friend, but by her inability to overcome an average case of embarrassment and teen angst.

Get over it, she had told herself. And yet she hadn't.

But Polly's reaction gave Caroline a glimmer of hope. Maybe her daughter sensed the gravity of the moment. Maybe what had happened to her all those years ago was at least awful enough to give her disaffected teenage daughter reason to pause. Like the years she had spent under the thumb of that one moment could be understood, at least a little, by someone other than herself.

"You never did anything about it?" Polly asked. "Never tried to get back at Emily? Or Ellie?"

"The retaliation gene must have skipped a generation," Caroline said. "I know it's hard for you to understand, but it was sort of like me against the world back then. My dad was gone. Grandma was a mess, working two jobs and starting to drink, so there was no one at home for me. When your best friend humiliates you in public and takes the rest of your friends with her . . . well, it's just easier to run away than fight. I know it's probably hard for someone like you to imagine, but I decided that it was easier to be invisible."

"Someone like me?"

"You're hardly invisible," Caroline said.

"I'm not exactly head cheerleader, either."

"But you have friends."

"Yeah, Kate and Peyton. And Peter, I guess. But if any of them did to me what Emily Kaplan did to you, I don't know what I'd do."

This surprised Caroline. If asked to name her daughter's friends, she would have immediately named Kate and Peyton, but she was surprised to realize that she'd be hard pressed to name more. And Peter? Who was Peter?

Caroline had always assumed that her daughter was well liked. She saw Polly's hairstyle, T-shirts, and tattoo as something that only a confident, socially adept teenager would attempt. Her articles in the school newspaper challenging the administration, her refusal to recite the Pledge of Allegiance in homeroom, and her success on the debate team had led Caroline to believe that her daughter was outspoken. Popular. (Did kids still use that word?) Maybe even admired. Kids with limited social standing, in her experience, tried to remain as nondescript as possible. Polly was anything but nondescript.

Then again, this was the longest conversation that she and Polly had had in almost two years. So really, what did she know?

"After the cafeteria," Caroline continued, "I wanted to crawl into a hole and hide. It's embarrassing to be alone, especially in high school. Embarrassing not to have friends to sit with. Embarrassing not to have a phone number to call when you can't remember the homework assignment. It makes you want to disappear. It's easier to let people forget you than remember you without any friends. Invisible was good. You don't strike me as wanting to be invisible."

"You have no clue what you're talking about," Polly said, her voice almost a whisper. "You have no idea how hard it is for me."

"Why don't you tell me?"

"I'm fine," Polly said, her voice flat. "It's not always easy, but nothing worth worrying about. Besides, you still haven't told me why we're driving to Grandma's house. What does Emily Kaplan and Ellie What's-her-face have to do with you breaking me out of school and dragging me to Massachusetts?"

Caroline took a deep breath. Her idea was ridiculous. Her plan was ridiculous. "I want to go find Emily Kaplan and say the things I should've said to her that day in the cafeteria."

Polly stared, her face blank.

Caroline waited for her daughter's reaction to shift. It didn't.

"That's it?" Polly asked, her eyes narrowing. "That's your plan?"

"Yes," Caroline said, trying her best to sound committed.

Polly leaned over the table a bit. "Mom," she said in a half whisper. "That's the stupidest thing I've ever heard."

It was almost 9:00 P.M. by the time they passed over the state line into Connecticut. Polly was hungry again. Caroline was tired. "I think we have a little more than three hours of driving still ahead of us," Caroline said. "Let's find a hotel to spend the night and get an early start in the morning, okay?"

"As long as it's not Motel 6."

Caroline raised an eyebrow.

"If the best they can do is leave the light on for me, the place must be a dump."

They stopped at a rest area along I-95 and ate cheeseburgers and fries at McDonald's. Their second meal eaten together today. Probably their second meal eaten together this month. And with actual conversation, too.

"Did you know the Queen of England owns a McDonald's?"

"That can't be right," Caroline said.

"The Google will prove me right," Polly said, pulling her phone from her coat pocket.

"No, it's fine. I believe you. I don't feel like another 'I told you so.' But that doesn't mean she eats the food."

"That lady? No way. Not that there's anything wrong with a little McDonald's from time to time. But I have to give queenie credit. She's got balls."

"Yeah?"

"Hell yeah," Polly said. "Can you imagine the nerve it must take to still be a queen in this day and age? It's got to be totally embarrassing by now. She gets to be queen *through birth*. Who does that today? It's like walking around topless in New York City."

"Huh?"

"It's totally legal to walk around topless in New York. Some woman actually made a ton of money by doing it and then suing the city when the cops arrested her."

"Okay," Caroline said. "But how is that like being the queen?"

"Both things are completely legal but completely ridiculous. Just because something's legal means it should be done. Imagine what would happen if Queen What's-her-face handed her crown over to the prime minister, declared Buckingham Palace an orphanage, and got a job driving taxicabs or something. People would love her for that. People would go ape shit over her for that."

"I don't think it's that easy," Caroline said.

"That's what people say when they don't have the nerve to do the right thing. She's the queen. Who better to end the completely embarrassing monarchy?"

"Oddly enough, I think you're probably right."

"You know I am." Polly was smiling as she stuffed her mouth with fries. Caroline couldn't remember the last time she had seen Polly smile at the dinner table.

"Speaking of doing the right thing," Polly said, her mouth still jammed with food, "don't you think you should call Dad? When you called him at the diner you told him that you'd call back soon. That was hours ago."

"I know, Polly. I know."

Caroline had told Tom not to worry. She told him she would call back soon. That had not gone over well.

"You do know," he'd said, "that saying 'don't worry' never stops anyone from worrying."

"I promise to call as soon as we stop," Caroline had assured him.

"You're stopped now," Tom said. "Take five minutes and tell me what's going on."

"Can you just trust me on this? I'll call as soon as I can."

"This isn't about trusting you. I just want to know why my wife and daughter are three hundred miles away from home."

"I'm fine. Polly's fine. Can't that be enough for now?"

"Do I have a choice?" One of those Tom questions that made you sound like a jerk no matter how you answered.

"No," she said. "You don't."

He had called her twice more since then. Both times Caroline had let the call go to voicemail. She knew that she needed to speak with him soon, and she also knew that she needed some privacy in order to have that conversation. Certainly out of earshot of Polly.

"Let's get supplies first," Caroline said. "Then I'll call."

The convenience store was attached to the rest area, so five minutes later, they were standing in front of a wire rack of T-shirts.

"I know they aren't what you normally wear, but it's just for bed. I swear I won't tell anyone about this."

"Why would anyone even wear something like this?" Polly asked. She removed a white shirt with an image of Connecticut across the chest. The message below the image read:

CONNECTICUT: TOO COOL FOR NEW ENGLAND.
TOO CLEAN FOR NEW YORK.

"It's not great," Caroline admitted.

"It's not even funny. It makes the person wearing it look like a douchebag. It actually makes New England and New York seem a lot better than Connecticut. And news flash: Connecticut is part of New England. This is possibly the stupidest T-shirt I've ever seen."

"Worse than your I'M NOT WITH STUPID ANYMORE T-shirt?"

It was a shirt that Polly had worn to her school's science fair last month. It showed a blue stick figure and a pink stick figure standing side by side. The pink stick figure had just punched the blue stick figure in the head. The small blue head was detached and flying away.

"That's a great shirt. I don't care what that stupid science fair judge said. It's funny. It's graphic. It's referential. And it actually makes fun of a legitimately stupid T-shirt. It's legitimate cultural commentary. It is nothing like this stupid shirt."

"Can you just find one to sleep in for tonight?"

Polly scanned the rack, shoving aside shirts as she rejected them.

Caroline sighed. "We can literally throw the shirt away when we're done sleeping in it. Burn it, even."

"Here," Polly said. "This is good." The shirt was white. It read WIKIPEDIA IS ACCURATE. Below this sentence, in parenthesis, it added, CITATION NEEDED.

"Yeah," Caroline said. "It's good."

"You don't even get it. Do you?"

"Not really," Caroline admitted. "But if you'll sleep in it tonight, that's all that matters."

Polly scanned the aisle. "How about some underwear?"

"I don't think we're going to find that in a convenience store."

"That would be a great product," Polly said, suddenly excited. "Don't you think?"

"Underwear?"

"No, like emergency underwear. Underwear in a can. Like the kind they put tennis balls in."

"I don't know, how often is someone stuck without underwear? Seems like a niche product."

"Maybe," Polly admitted. "Still, it sounds good. So I guess I'm going commando tonight?"

"Unless we find a store first."

"That's fine," Polly said. "Some people believe it's healthier not to wear underwear. Doctors even."

Caroline sighed. "Sometimes I hate the Internet."

By the time they stepped off the elevator and walked the dozen paces to their hotel room, it was nearly 10:00 P.M. Caroline was exhausted. The excitement she had experienced upon leaving the diner had given way to uncertainty and a looming sense of dread. Even with Polly tepidly onboard, Caroline's spirits were ebbing. She was beginning to feel foolish for even attempting this trip. She worried that tomorrow she might feel downright stupid.

Sleep, she hoped, would make things better.

She slid the plastic room key into the lock and pushed the door open.

"I thought you said nonsmoking," Polly said as she sat down on the bed. "This place totally reeks."

"Someone must have ignored the no smoking signs," Caroline said, pointing to the placard on the nightstand.

"Mom. It's awful."

Caroline thought about debating the point but reconsidered. "I'll see if I can get us another room." She picked up the phone and dialed zero.

"Good evening," a female voice answered. "May I help you?"

"Yes, hello. This is Caroline Jacobs in room 208. I requested a nonsmoking room, and this room smells of cigarette smoke."

"Reeks of cigarette smoke," Polly said.

"Room 208?" the woman said.

"Yes."

"Room 208 is a nonsmoking room."

"Yes, I appreciate that," Caroline said. "Nevertheless, the room does smell of cigarette smoke."

"Reeks!" Polly shouted.

"In fact, the whole floor is nonsmoking," the woman said. "A previous guest may have violated our policy, but that room is supposed to be nonsmoking."

"Yes, I know that the room is *supposed* to be nonsmoking, but the smell is bad. Could we be moved to another room, please?"

"Just a moment, please." A clicking of computer keys, a momentary pause, and then, "I'm afraid I don't have another nonsmoking room available with two beds, Mrs. Jacobs. I could put you in a single and have a cot moved into the room if you'd like."

Caroline looked back at Polly, who was scanning the available television stations on a laminated card. "Let me call you back. Okay?"

Caroline hung up the phone. "They don't have any doubles left. We can stay here or they can move us to a single and get us a cot. What do you think?"

"Seriously?" Polly said. "We stay in this disgusting room or I sleep on a cot? That's our choice?"

"I'll sleep on the cot. It's not a big deal."

Polly shook her head.

"I'm going to use the bathroom. Let me know what you want to do when I get out."

Caroline was suddenly worried. She and Polly had been enjoying themselves for the past couple hours. There had been banter. She and Polly had been *bantering.* Speaking without sarcasm. Communicating without contempt. It hadn't exactly been a profound conversation, but the fact that they were speaking at all was amazing. The room situation had put everything in jeopardy. She and Polly were standing atop a shaky pedestal, shifting back and forth in order to maintain balance. It sounded stupid, but she knew that something as simple as a smelly hotel room might be enough to knock them over. Restore their routine.

She was unbuttoning her jeans when she heard Polly's voice in the other room.

"Hello, this is Caroline Jacobs in room 208 again. May I ask who I'm speaking to?"

"Polly?" Caroline shouted. She quickly rebuttoned her jeans and pulled open the bathroom door.

"Are you in charge this evening, or is there someone above you in the chain of command?"

Polly placed a finger over her lips in a vaguely conspiratorial gesture. "Perfect," she said. As she moved her finger away from her mouth, Caroline saw that her daughter was grinning. "Here's the problem: I paid for a nonsmoking double and you put me in a room that reeks of cigarette smoke. And now I've been offered a single and a cot in exchange. This is not acceptable."

Caroline opened her mouth to speak but Polly appeared to anticipate this, widening her eyes in disapproval and holding up an index finger to signal that she needed a minute. In that moment, Caroline saw her own mother in those green eyes and that snap of disapproval.

"Hold on, Tina," Polly said. "I'm not finished. Here is what I will do. If I am not placed in a nonsmoking double or better, I will be placing a call to the Holiday Inn corporate offices tonight. I don't think anyone will answer, but I'll leave a message on as many voicemails as I can find. Then I'll get online and start talking about how my asthmatic daughter is being forced to sleep in a room that smells of cigarette smoke. I'll e-mail every organization I can find that deals with children with asthma, and then I'll ask my ten thousand Twitter followers to retweet my posts. You know how social media works. Right?"

Polly paused a moment, still grinning and then said, "Sure. Call me back." She hung up the phone.

"Polly!" Caroline said. "What do you expect them to do? Build us a nonsmoking room?"

"Gimme a break. They'll find something."

"I didn't know you have a Twitter account."

"I don't. Twitter's for assholes. Just trust me, Mom. I know what I'm doing."

"You don't have any idea what you're doing. You're fifteen years old, for God's sake."

"Just trust me. Please?"

As if to offer Polly support, the phone rang.

"This is Caroline Jacobs," Polly said, flashing a smile at her mother. Polly listened for a moment and then said, "That will be perfect, Tina. Thank you. And I'm sorry I had to be so bitchy. I just get a little crazy when it comes to my daughter."

Another longer pause and then Polly said, "Perfect. Thank you. You've been very helpful."

"What?" Caroline said, trying to hide her grudging admiration.

"We've been upgraded to one of their executive suites. Someone will be up here in a second with our new keycards."

Caroline just stared. Despite her overly earnest, aw-shucks father and her uncertain, nonconfrontational mother, Polly had somehow grown into a person who could manage people and solve problems with efficiency and ease. She reminded Caroline of Tiffany. Okay, Polly's ability to lie with so little effort was troubling, but she had also managed to exhibit more self-confidence and nerve than Caroline had exhibited in most of her life.

"You've really become your own person," she said.

"What did you expect me to do? Become another you?"

"Hey!"

"I'm not saying that you're lame or anything. You're not half bad. And if I'm ever a mom someday, I'd totally want to be like you. At least try to."

"Yeah?" A smile filled Caroline's face.

"Don't let it go to your head."

"No chance of that," Caroline said.

"And even though I'd want to marry someone way cooler than Dad, at least you guys are still married. It's more than I can say for most of my friends' parents. It's kind of cool. I hope my husband is still into me when I'm as old as you."

"As old as me?"

"You know what I mean."

She did.

"And you take great pictures," Polly said. "You're totally wasting your talent, but at least you got some."

"Thanks," Caroline said. She felt herself blushing and turned away.

"But Mom, you can be such a pushover."

"I know," Caroline said. Her smile had diminished, but it was still there. "And I'm glad you're not. It's just—it's strange how a person can become something so unlike either of her parents."

Polly smiled. "Henry Shrapnel's father was a vicar."

"What did his mother do?"

"That was like two hundred years ago. She was a housewife. Women couldn't exactly have careers back then."

Some don't exactly have careers even today, Caroline wanted to say.

"So?" Polly said. "Are you impressed? With the new room, I mean."

"You got us the room, but it wasn't right," Caroline said, more out of a sense of parental duty than genuine belief. "You can't just lie to people to get your way."

"And Tina can't just stick us in a smoking room or make one of us sleep on a cot. They should have upgraded us when you first called."

She couldn't argue with that.

"I'd tell you to get your bag packed," Polly said, "but we still don't have any clothes."

"We'll get some tomorrow. Okay?" she said. "No, forget the *okay*. We'll get them tomorrow. No more complaining."

"I was just kidding. Geez, what's your deal? I just got you into an executive suite. I'd think you would be happy."

"I am," Caroline said. In fact, she couldn't remember a time when she had been happier.

ten

When Caroline left the room, Polly was lying on the bed, watching a movie on an enormous flat-screen television and eating a bowl of ice cream—compliments of the management. She was still gloating, and rightfully so.

Caroline needed to call Tom. But she also needed her own victory. That's why she was seated here, in an armchair chosen for its stain resistance, in front of a fireplace never designed to hold a flame, listening to music that was written for its propensity to be forgotten. She chose this spot in the lobby because she was well out of earshot from the comatose desk clerk. A perfect spot to call Wendy.

It was late, but Caroline knew her friend would answer. Wendy possessed the energy of a thousand angry bulls and was up at all hours of the night.

"Sorry, my arms were full," Wendy said, a little out of breath. "What's up?"

"Hi," said, Caroline, pushing back with pleasantries. Her simple "What's up?" already felt judgmental. "How are you?"

"I'm fine. Just bringing in some groceries. What's up?"

"You're going to think I'm crazy," Caroline said, feeling more foolish by the second. "Maybe I should just go."

"All the more reason to talk. Tell me what's going on." Caroline could practically hear her friend settling in an armchair, ready for a good story.

"Okay," she said. "But no laughing." Caroline took a deep breath and told Wendy about the events of the past twenty-four hours: the PTO debacle, her extraction of Polly from the clutches of Mr. Powers, their upgrade to the executive suite, even the apparent similarities between the Queen of England and topless women in New York City. "If Polly could con someone into giving us some clean clothes, we'd be all set."

"I don't get it. You broke Polly out of jail so you could visit your mom?"

"Not exactly."

"Good, because as a story, that sucks."

"I wasn't finished," Caroline said.

"Then finish already."

"Remember Emily Kaplan?"

"Of course," Wendy said. "What kind of friend do you think I am?"

"I'm going back to Blackstone to confront her."

In the silence that followed, Caroline could see her friend's nose wrinkle and her eyes narrow to slits. Her confused look. The one she'd seen a million times before. "To what—?"

"To tell her off."

There was a longer pause. Three full seconds this time. Three endless seconds to allow Caroline to come to grips with how completely insane her plan sounded.

"Are you serious?" Wendy finally said.

"Am I crazy?"

"Yes," Wendy replied. "Bat shit crazy. Loony toons. Certifiable. But—"

"But . . . ?" Caroline repeated hopefully.

"I kind of love the idea, too."

"You do?"

"Yeah," Wendy said. "Who doesn't want to get revenge on their high school bully?"

There it was. The b-word again.

"She wasn't exactly a bully," Caroline said, defending Emily once more.

"Don't be stupid. She was a total bully."

"I don't know if what she did qualifies as bullying."

"What is wrong with you?" Wendy asked. "Emily Kaplan was the worst kind of bully. She was a bully with a smile. She isolated you."

"I don't know if that makes her a bully."

"Why are you defending her?"

"I don't know," Caroline said. "I just think, well, that I probably played a part in everything that happened, too. It wasn't all Emily. She wasn't *required* to be my friend."

"You're an idiot. If that had happened today, Emily would be sitting in the principal's office with her parents. Kids kill themselves over shit like this. You didn't lose your friends. She stole them from you. All of them."

"So you don't think it's a bad idea? Going back to find her?"

"I didn't say that. I think it's a great idea, but it might be a great bad idea. I'm worried that it sounds better than it actually is."

"Now you've lost me."

"I assume that Emily still lives in Blackstone?"

"Yes," Caroline said.

"Figures."

"Meaning . . . ?"

"Meaning people like Emily never leave their hometowns. As long as she stays in Blackstone, she'll always be the goddamn prom queen. If she ever moved, she'd just be the girl who likes to tell everyone that she was once the prom queen."

"Okay." Caroline didn't argue the point.

"So let's say you find her and tell her off. Tell her to go to hell. Tell her that she was a bitch in high school. What does that get you?"

"Satisfaction?"

"Only if your words hurt her in some way," Wendy said. "If

she just fires back and calls you a loser or tells you to fuck off and walks away, what good was the trip?"

"Do you think I'm pathetic for even thinking this was a good idea?"

"Of course I don't. Caroline, you are one of the best people I know. You're smart and honest and kind. You're a good mother to Polly, which—you and I know—can't be easy at times. And you've got a great marriage. A great husband."

"Thanks, Wen—"

"Don't interrupt me. You're gifted, too. If you'd stop being such a coward and let me see more of your pictures, I think I'd find that you're a more talented photographer that I've seen already."

Caroline warmed inside. "Thanks," she said quietly.

"So we've had the Hallmark moment. Back to Emily Kaplan." Caroline laughed. This was the Wendy she knew and loved. "What if she tells you to fuck off? What if she just walks away? Do you feel any better then?"

"I don't know. But I know that at this moment, I feel good."

"Okay," Wendy said, sounding less than convinced. "I just don't want this to go bad for you. It really is a little crazy."

"I know."

"What does Polly think of it?"

"She thinks I'm nuts, too," Caroline said. "But it's better than getting suspended. And I think she sees it as an adventure. We're actually getting along a little."

"But if it doesn't last, just remember: It's not you. Teenage girls are fickle. And despicable."

"You're telling me?" Caroline laughed a little. "Anyway, who knows? Maybe she's finally coming out the other side."

"Maybe," Wendy said, sounding unconvinced. "And I think it's great that she's with you. Just don't screw this up."

"Thanks for the vote of confidence."

"I'm serious," Wendy said. "This is the kind of thing that works well in the movies but bombs in real life. Just be ready for that."

"Even if I bomb, at least I tried."

"Sure. I can just hear you saying that after Emily skewers you and sends you home in tears. *At least I tried!* Rainbows and kittens."

"You don't have a lot of faith in me," Caroline said.

"I have plenty of faith in you. But I have plenty of faith in Emily Kaplan, too. If she's anything like she was in high school, you'll have your hands full."

eleven

"How's your king-sized bed?" Polly asked across the darkened room. "Better than a stupid cot?"

Caroline could hear the smile in her daughter's voice.

"It's not bad," Caroline said. "A little lumpy, but it'll do for one night."

"Yeah, right."

"You did a good job," Caroline said. "Better than I could've done."

"Better than you *did*," Polly said.

"Where did you learn how to do that anyway?" she asked.

"Geez, Mom. Watch a movie sometime. Read a blog. It wasn't exactly rocket science."

"I'm not talking about what you did." (Though that had impressed her more than she was willing to admit.) "I meant *how you did it*. You certainly didn't get nerve like that from me. Or your father for that matter."

Silence filled the darkened room. Caroline decided not to press further. She closed her eyes.

"I sometimes wonder if I'm the person I'm supposed to be," Polly said. He voice was quiet. Almost distant. "Or if I'm just filling the only role left over."

Whoa.

Polly had just shared something from the inside, a place where Caroline had been shut out for years. She'd have to choose her next words carefully, afraid to say the wrong thing. After a second of debate, she opted for a nonthreatening "Huh?"

"Dad always says that I was a late bloomer. Maybe that explains it a little. I feel like by the time I was ready to be the person I was supposed to be, all the good jobs were taken."

Caroline waited for Polly to continue, hoping that silence would serve as a sufficient prompt. When it didn't, she said, "Jobs?" trying to achieve the perfect blend of casual interest and disinterest—just enough to let her daughter know she wasn't being interrogated.

"Not jobs exactly," Polly said. "Roles. Like parts in a play. All the good parts were taken. The pretty girl parts. The jocks. Even the genius kids who'll go to Harvard or Yale someday. Those parts were filled, too. I got left filling in the little parts. The ones no one else wanted."

"Like what?" Caroline asked, fearing that the wrong question would shut her daughter down completely.

"The smart-ass," Polly said. "The hard-ass." After a moment, she added, "The pain in the ass."

The smile was gone from Polly's voice.

"It's not that I don't like my part," she said. "I like it a lot. The articles in the school newspaper. My newsletter. The protests. The debate team. I believe in those things. I like who I am. But I would've liked the chance to be one of the pretty girls, too. I mean, isn't there a place in the pretty girl clique for a short brunette? I don't mean to sound superficial, but sometimes I just want to be pretty."

It was as if Polly were speaking to both Caroline and herself at the same time.

"And I know I could've been one of the smart girls. The ones who sit in the front of the class and nod whenever the teacher is talking. I'm smart enough, but there's more to it than that, and it doesn't really come naturally to me. Like last week when Emma Cobb asked Mr. Drake if she could do extra credit right after Zachary asked for an extension on his midterm—the one that's due in a couple of days. Emma knows that the best time to shine is right after someone acts like an idiot, so her extra-credit question was worth two or three times more than it would have been. Because she knew when to ask. I'm not socially awkward or anything, but I feel like it takes me a little longer to figure those kinds of things out."

"That's really how you feel?" Caroline said, astonished.

"Yeah, I do. Dad always says I'm just finding my own way. You think I'm crazy. Grandma says I'm an agitator. Mr. Cronin once called me an anarchist, and even though I know he was kidding, I think he was only half kidding."

Caroline laughed. It was true. She did think that Polly was crazy. At least a little.

"The problem is there's only room for one anarchist per school. So kids respect me, but they don't think of me as friendship material."

"I'm sorry, honey." Caroline was trying hard to conceal the devastation she felt.

Polly plowed forward. "All of it leaves me wondering: Am I a lonely anarchist because I was supposed to be a lonely anarchist, or was that just the crack I managed to squeeze into when parts were being chosen? Was that all there was left for me? And what if I'd found a seat at Misty Dean's table at lunch during that first week of school? Would I be a popular girl instead? Or if I hadn't forgotten about field hockey tryouts when I was a freshman, would I be a sporty girl now? Maybe I didn't need to be the person who worries about equal funding for the girls' soccer team. I don't even like soccer."

Caroline opened her mouth to speak but Polly seemed to anticipate this.

"Don't worry, Mom. It was a rhetorical question. I'm not looking for you to tackle any major philosophical questions tonight."

"Thanks for talking to me about it," Caroline said, breathing a sigh of relief. "It means a lot that you told me."

"I figured I owed you. You told me about Emily Kaplan, so I thought I should throw you a bone."

"Throw me a bone?"

"Yeah," Polly said. The smile had returned to her face. "I wasn't going to tell you about losing my virginity or anything like that. But I thought I owed you something."

"Gee, thanks," Caroline said, praying that the virginity comment was just a joke.

twelve

In an ideal world, Caroline would've driven directly to Emily Kaplan's house, knocked on her front door, said what she had to say, and left town without her mother ever knowing that she had ever been there.

This world was anything but ideal.

Caroline's mother had mentioned months ago that Emily was still living in Blackstone. "She owns that goddamn knickknack store," she had said. But Caroline didn't know where Emily Kaplan, whose last name was no longer Kaplan, lived. She would need her mother to provide that information, and that would not come without many questions.

Questions Caroline wanted to avoid.

Penelope Waters still lived in the same small house on Main Street that she had moved into with her daughters after her husband had left. She had transformed the shabby rental into one of the better homes on the street—only now, it wasn't a rental. Penelope bought it after Caroline had finished school. She had put the house together, as she had put her life back together, bit by bit. With a lot of work and what Caroline assumed had been a significant financial investment, the house no longer resembled the run-down eyesore that had embarrassed Caroline as a teenager. The house, which now served as her mother's place of business as well as her home, abutted the Blackstone River. What was once a trash-strewn embankment leading to the water had been transformed into a gentle, rocky slope. The house itself—red with white shutters—was surrounded by a pristine front lawn and immaculate landscaping. A wide front porch, another post-Caroline addition, gave the home a welcoming air. Caroline often wondered why her mother had chosen to remain here when she could've moved to a better home in a better location long ago. She suspected it had something to do with Lucy.

Caroline pulled into the driveway, maneuvering her car alongside a black minivan and her mother's Buick. For a moment, she considered turning around and coming back later. The minivan was undoubtedly a customer's car. And Caroline hated to be around when her mother was working.

Not Polly. She leaned forward in her seat. "Oh good!" she said. "Maybe Nana has a customer."

"I'll never understand your fascination with her business," Caroline said.

"You should be proud of Nana. She's doing something she totally made up. She's like an inventor. Like Steve Jobs or that asshole, Thomas Edison."

"No kidding," Caroline said, thinking about Tom's odd assemblage of careers. No one in her family seemed to be able to hold down a normal job. "Wait. Thomas Edison was an asshole?"

"Mom, he used to electrocute elephants just to prove that his electrical system was better than Tesla's."

"Was it?"

"If it was really better, would he be electrocuting elephants?"

"Good point," she said. "And by the way, Steve Jobs was kind of an asshole, too."

"I'll give you that. But he didn't murder pachyderms."

Polly rang the bell. The door opened a moment later to reveal a sixty-five-year old woman who looked and moved as if she were at least fifteen years younger. Penelope Waters had short, blond hair, a petite figure and a perpetual smile, which was bizarre, because when Caroline was growing up, her mother had rarely smiled, never laughed, and did everything she could to avoid conversation. Caroline understood her mother's depression. She had been depressed herself. But she couldn't help but resent her mother's miraculous resurgence after she had left for college. She was a person who Caroline barely recognized. In many ways, she no longer felt like she knew the woman who had once been her mother.

"Hi, Nana!" Polly said, stepping into the kitchen.

"Your mother didn't tell me you were coming, too."

"I didn't?" Caroline said.

"You most certainly didn't. Not that it's a big deal. I'm always happy to see my Polymath! She can sleep on the pullout."

"Polymath?"

"It's what I started calling her last time she stayed with me."

"I hate to ask," Caroline said. "But what's a polymath?"

"Mom's kind of the opposite of a polymath," Polly said.

"Don't be mean," Caroline's mother said. "A polymath is someone who knows a lot about a lot of things. Polly is like a walking talking Internet."

"I wouldn't go that far," Polly said. "I just remember the good stuff."

"I wish you would've remembered to tell me you were coming," Caroline's mother said.

"Sorry," Caroline said. "I didn't mean to not tell you. And we might not be staying overnight anyway."

"Mom has a lot on her mind," Polly said with a wry smile. "She's plotting revenge."

"Really?" Her mother sounded overly invested already. "Revenge against who?"

"No one," Caroline said.

"Emily Kaplan," Polly said. "The Wicked Bitch of the West."

"Polly!" Caroline said.

"What is she talking about?" her mother asked.

"Can I please take off my coat before you start grilling me?"

"Fine. I have a customer in the living room anyway. We're almost finished. Put your things in the guest room and come join us. You might be of some help."

The guest room had once been Caroline's childhood bedroom, though nothing of her childhood remained. It was on the second floor, directly across the hall from the bedroom that had once belonged to Lucy. The door to her sister's bedroom was shut, as it always was.

Caroline and Polly removed their coats and tossed their belongings onto the bed. Polly picked up the teddy bear placed on the center of the bed. "Was this yours when you were a kid?"

"Nope. Purely decorative."

"Nana went to a store and bought a decorative teddy bear?"

"I guess so."

Polly scanned the room. "Is anything in here left over from when you were a kid?"

Caroline took a second to inventory the contents of the room. "I don't think so."

"Isn't that weird?" Polly asked. "Losing your room to a bunch of future guests?"

"Not weird," Caroline said. "Sad, though."

"Sounds weird to me," Polly said. "Growing up sucks."

Caroline agreed but didn't say so. She used the bathroom, spending an extra minute or two in front of the sink, washing her hands and fiddling with her hair. After stalling for as long as possible, she succumbed to Polly's pleas and the two of them made their way down the stairs and into the living room.

Caroline's mother was sitting on the edge of the couch, leaning forward. Sitting in the love seat opposite was a thin, pale man in his thirties. His hands were folded in his lap, and he was sitting stock straight, which made him look like an altar boy during a Sunday morning service. A glass coffee table filled the space between the man and her mother. Atop the table were a box of tissues and two small, wooden boxes.

Caroline's mother rose. "Caroline, Polly—this is George Durrow. George, this is my daughter, Caroline, and my granddaughter, Polly."

"It's nice to meet you," Polly said, waving a hand and offering a smile.

George Durrow nodded in their direction and returned his gaze to the two wooden boxes in front of him.

"George is trying to decide upon a vessel. He's narrowed his choice down to two. I thought maybe you could help him. Offer another perspective."

Polly took the seat on the couch beside George Durrow and lifted the wooden box closest to her off the table. It was about the size of a shoe box, made from a dark, red wood and was decorated with inlays of roses and a crucifix on the lid.

"Who did you lose?" Polly asked.

Durrow turned and stared at Polly for a moment, appearing to size up the girl sitting beside him. "Her name was Tutu." He paused for another moment and then added, "She was a cockatoo."

"I'm so sorry for your loss," Polly said.

George Durrow's gaze returned to the box still sitting on the table. He lifted it and began turning it over in his hands. It was made from the same red wood as the one Polly had. "I like that one a lot," Polly said.

"Yeah?" Durrow asked.

"Yeah. I always like the ones without any religious stuff on them. There's no way of knowing how our pets felt about God, so I always think it's better to play it safe and keep God and Jesus and all that other junk off the vessel."

"You can call it a coffin," Durrow said. "It's okay. I mean, that's what it is."

"Coffin, then," Polly said, smiling back. "I like that coffin a lot. Are you having a memorial service, too?"

"Just a private burial," Durrow said, his gaze shifting down to his sneakers. "Just me and Tutu." He swallowed hard. "People never think of birds the same way as dogs or cats. They'd think a service would be silly."

"Which is ridiculous," Polly said. "Since birds can live a lot longer than dogs or cats."

"Exactly," Durrow said, his smile returning. "My parents gave me Tutu when I was eight years old. That was almost thirty years ago. Tutu outlived my mother."

"I don't think there's anything wrong with wanting a service for Tutu," Polly said. "If it's what you want, you should just do it. Fuck the people who think it's silly."

Caroline wanted to reprimand Polly for her use of language, but the ever widening smile on George Durrow's face stopped her in her tracks.

"I'll take this one," he said, passing the wooden box to Penelope.

"Okay, George," she said. "I like it, too. Will there be anything else?"

"Can we make an appointment for next week?" he asked. "After the burial?"

"Of course. I'm going to need a few minutes to finish up the paperwork and give you a final total, so we can put something on the calendar after I'm finished. Okay?"

"Sure," Durrow said. "No rush. Would you like me to come back later to settle things? When your family isn't here?"

"No, it won't take but a few minutes."

"Do you have a plot picked out?" Polly asked.

"Yes, we did that first," Durrow said, smiling again.

"Can I see it?" she asked.

"Sure," he said. "Is it all right with you, Penny?"

"Of course. I'll have everything ready when you get back."

Polly and Durrow rose. "We can go through the back door," Polly said. "Right, Nana?"

"Of course," she said. "Just lead the way for Mr. Durrow."

Polly and Durrow left the room as Penelope flipped through several sheets of paper on her lap. "That poor man," she said. "Birds are the worst. No one understands how attached a person can get to a bird. Did you hear what George said? He and Tutu had been together since he was a kid."

"Yeah, it's a shame," Caroline said, trying to sound sincere but knowing she did not. "I still can't believe how seriously Polly takes this stuff. I know you told me that she was good at it, but I'd never seen her in action before."

"It's not hard, Caroline," her mother said. "You just have to be willing to accept death as a part of life."

"That must be it," Caroline said flatly. "I can't accept death."

"It's not funny," her mother said.

"I never said it was."

"I'm serious," her mother said. "I can't remember the last time I heard you say her name."

"I'm not the one preserving her bedroom like some museum exhibit."

"What's wrong with wanting to keep the memory of my daughter alive? It's not as if I'm pressed for space. Maybe if you set foot in there sometime, you would understand what it feels like to be able to stand in your sister's presence again."

"That's not my sister," Caroline said, pointing in the direction of Lucy's bedroom. "It's just a collection of old toys and furniture and clothing. It's no different than those headstones in the back-yard. It's like a big, furnished gravestone up there."

"There's nothing wrong with spending a little time visiting the dead. You should try it sometime."

"She has a gravestone," Caroline said. "If I want to visit her, that's where I'll go. Not into a bedroom filled with Barbie dolls and Baby-Sitters Club books."

Caroline stared a moment at her mother. How they had found themselves down this road again, and so quickly?

Her mother rose from the desk. "Lucy," she said.

"What?" Caroline snapped.

"Lucy," her mother repeated. "Your sister's name was Lucy. In case you forgot."

Caroline turned and left the room.

thirteen

"This is why you came home? To get even with a high school friend for something she said to you twenty years ago?" Penelope asked.

"I know," Polly said, her mouth half full of turkey sandwich. "Can you believe it? It's like the most badass thing that Mom's ever done."

They were sitting at a small kitchen table, eating sandwiches off paper plates and drinking lemonade from tall glasses. Caroline had finally explained the purpose of their trip to her mother. She had tried to leave out the details of the cafeteria incident, glossing over the event with a few simple sentences, but Polly would have none of it, quickly filling in the gaps that Caroline was trying to avoid. Polly loved the story, sharing each detail as if it was a tiny treasure.

"I don't know why you're smiling," Caroline said to Polly. "There's nothing funny about this at all."

"I don't think it's funny," Polly said. "I think it's freakin' amazing. I thought it was crazy last night, but now I'm all in."

"I'm not trying to be funny," Caroline said. "And I'm not trying to be amazing. It's just something I need to do. It's been hanging over my head for too long."

"So you're going to knock on Emily's door and tell her that she was mean to you in high school," Penelope said. "Then, what—demand an apology?"

"I think she should punch the bitch in the nose!" Polly said, bits of turkey and cheese flying from her mouth.

"Polly!" Caroline and Penelope snapped in unison.

Polly directed her attention to the potato chips on her plate, a reaction that Caroline knew was more in response to her grandmother's disapproval than her own.

"I don't know what I'm going to say when I get to Emily's house," Caroline said. "Not exactly, at least. But I'll figure it out when I get there."

"You should knock on the door instead of ringing the bell," Polly said. "It's totally more aggressive."

"Caroline, really . . . you were just kids," her mother said. "You don't actually think you can blame a woman for something she did when she was fifteen? Do you?"

"Why can't she?" Polly asked.

"Kids do stupid things," Penelope said. "That's the way of the world."

"I'm a kid," Polly said. "Are you saying that everything I do today won't mean anything when I get old? Because if that's true, I should just do whatever I want, since no one's going to hold it against me."

"That's not what I meant," Penelope said. "I just think that twenty-five years is too long to hold a grudge. Emily is an entirely different person today."

"That's bullshit," Caroline fired back. Polly stared at her mother, her mouth hanging open. There was disbelief in her eyes. Maybe a little pride, too.

"I'm sorry," Caroline said, feeling like the teenager at the table again.

"No, go on," her mother said. "I'd like to hear this."

"Yeah, go on," Polly said.

But Caroline didn't want to explain. She wanted to keep moving forward before inertia overtook her and brought this pilgrimage to a halt. The more she explained, the less certain she felt. For once in her life, she wanted to act from her gut instead of her head.

"This is just something I have to do," she said, rising from her chair. "That's all. So can you tell me where she lives so we can get this done?"

"We?" her mother asked. "Who exactly is going over to the Emily's house?"

"Me and Polly," Caroline said.

"You're bringing Polly?"

"I just drove a thousand miles without a change of underwear," Polly said. "I'm going."

"I promised she could come."

This wasn't entirely true. They hadn't discussed the actual logistics, but Caroline wasn't about to admit that she needed her daughter. That somehow Polly radiated the strength she lacked.

"You promised her?" her mother said. "That's your reason?"

"It's important to keep your promises, Nana," Polly said.

"Polly, you're my only grandchild and I love you very much, but shut up."

Caroline stood her ground. "Mom, I just need you to let me do this without giving me a hard time. Maybe it's a mistake, but it's one you need to let me make."

Caroline was still searching for that perfect comeback when she and Polly were in the car, on the final leg of their journey. Just a few more miles between her and insanity.

She was surprised at how calm she felt. Even unprepared, Caroline knew that she would have the upper hand. Emily had no idea that history was about to chase her down. As difficult as it would be to confront her former friend, it would be an even greater shock to Emily. At least that's what Caroline told herself.

"Why did you swear at Nana?" Polly asked.

"What?"

"I've never heard you swear in your life, and now you're cursing at your own mother."

"I didn't swear," Caroline said.

"Yes, you did. She said that you shouldn't blame Emily because she's a different person today, and you said that was bullshit."

"Fine," Caroline admitted. "I swore. I was angry."

"But I've never heard you swear. Ever."

"I know," Caroline said. "I'm sorry. I'm swearing a lot this week."

"But do you really think it's bullshit?"

"Yes," Caroline said. "I do. I think it's bullshit."

"How come?"

Caroline thought for a moment, uncertain about how honest she wanted to be with her daughter.

"There's no great dividing line between being a kid and an adult. We're not all caterpillars turning into butterflies. You are what you are. When you grow up, you may be more careful than when you were a kid. You don't say what you think as much as you once did. You learn to play nice. But you're still the same person who did good things or rotten things when you were young. Whether you feel good about them or bad . . . whether you regret them. Well, that's a different thing. But it's not like they disappear forever."

"So you don't think Emily has changed at all?"

"Not really. I mean, she might know that what she did was wrong, but I think she probably knew that day, too. She knew how terrible it was to leave me standing there. And then to keep ignoring me every day after that? That was the worst. Whether she knew it then or knows it now, she's responsible for what happened."

"So you would still think that Emily is a bitch even if she adopted a hundred kids from Ethiopia or found the cure for chlamydia?"

"Chlamydia?"

"Relax," Polly said. "We learned about it in health."

Caroline smiled. "All I know is that I'm the same person I was in high school. I know a little more and I've done a little more, but I'm essentially the same person. I didn't suddenly become something different when I became an adult. And part of me is the result of what happened in the cafeteria that day and all those days after. A big part."

"Is that why you're doing this? You don't want Emily to be a big part of you anymore?"

"I guess that's a good way to explain it," Caroline said.

"Too bad," Polly said. "I liked your revenge reason better."

"Oh, don't worry. There's revenge mixed in there, too."

Polly smiled. "Good."

Wendy was right. Prom queens never did stray far from home. In the case of Emily Kaplan-turned-Labonte (Emily had married her high school sweetheart), she lived about a half mile from the high school. The Labontes lived on Summer Street, in a large colonial set on the top of a flat hill in a new subdivision that hadn't existed when Caroline lived in Blackstone. The house was surrounded by a lawn of uniform green. Not a single brown patch or crabgrass blemish to be found. The mulch in the beds surrounding the house was red, and the shrubs and flowers were meticulously maintained. A wide porch wrapped around the house in one great, big architectural embrace; a harvest wreath hung on the front door. The driveway—long, smooth, and dark—ended at a three-car garage, nearly the size of Caroline's entire home. A Plexiglas basketball hoop adorned the garage, as did a distressed sign in black and gold that read WAHROONGA.

Caroline brought the car to a stop on the side of the road and turned off the engine.

"What the hell is a Wahroonga?" Polly asked.

"I think it's the name of the house."

"Who names their house?"

"I guess Emily and Randy do," Caroline said, finding this fact surprisingly reassuring.

"What a couple of idiots," Polly said.

Tension crept into every muscle of Caroline's body. She tried to relax, tipping her head left and right to loosen the muscles in her neck. She took several deep breaths, exhaling through her mouth each time. The pressure only grew. She knew she needed to go now before it got any worse.

"Are you okay?" Polly asked. "You're acting like a freak."

"I'm fine. Time to go."

"Wait. Just wait a second. Do you know how NASA plans on saving the Earth if an asteroid is ever coming our way?"

"Huh?"

"An asteroid," Polly repeated. "Like the one that killed the di-nosaurs. Do you know how NASA wants to stop it from hitting the planet?"

"Bruce Willis?"

"No. And that movie sucked. It's actually much easier. All they have to do is send a rocket up and park it next to the asteroid. Everything has gravity. Me. You. The killer asteroid. The rocket. If they park the rocket next to the asteroid early enough, it will start to pull the asteroid toward it with its gravity. Only a teeny-tiny amount, but a teeny-tiny amount becomes a whole lot if you have enough time. And a zillion miles to work with."

"Okay, Polymath," Caroline said. "Why the astronomy lesson?"

"That's what Emily did to you. If you're sitting here, starting to think that what she did wasn't a big deal, remember that rocket parked next to the asteroid. Maybe she nudged you off course a tiny bit, but you've been off course ever since. That tiny bit has become a lot. You went way off course because of her."

"Why are you telling me this?"

"Because I don't want you to let her off the hook. I don't want you to forget what she did to you. Bullies always get away with stuff. All the time. But not this time."

Caroline smiled. "Thanks, hon. Now wait here."

"What?"

"I need you to stay in the car."

"You can't be serious," Polly snapped.

"I am serious. This is as far as you go. I can't have you standing over my shoulder when I knock on that door."

"No way, I'm going."

"No you're not," Caroline said.

"This is bullshit," Polly said. The anger that Caroline had become accustomed to was back in force. "I didn't come all this way to wait in the car. I'm not a dog."

"Don't be ridiculous. You know you can't come with me."

"Why not?"

"Put yourself in my shoes," Caroline said. "Would you want your teenage daughter standing next to you if you were me? How would that look?"

"I won't say a word. I'll just stand there."

"Polly."

"I'll maintain a safe distance. You won't even know I'm there. Think of me like Odysseus tied to that mast. I won't get involved at all. I'll just listen."

Polly was bargaining. Caroline knew it. Her daughter's anger had been replaced, as quickly as it had arisen, by the grudging realization that her mother was right. She knew it would be a bad idea to tag along, but still, she wanted to be there when Emily opened that door. She wanted to be there when her mother let her high school bully have it.

Caroline loved her for it.

"I know you wouldn't say anything," Caroline said. "But if I'm going to do what I should've done a long time ago, I need to do it alone."

"But I came all this way," Polly said, sounding much younger and a little sad. "It's not fair."

"I know," Caroline said. "I don't think I'd be sitting in this driveway if you hadn't come with me. But I have to do this last part on my own. You know that."

Polly looked away, turning her attention to the house. Angry resignation.

"Wait," Caroline said. "I can let you listen in."

"How?"

"Call my phone. I'll answer it and stick it in my pocket. I don't know how much you'll be able to hear, but at least it will be something."

A marginal smile, one that Caroline knew her daughter was fighting every inch of the way, crept across her face. "Fine," she said. "But this still totally sucks."

"I know. Wish me luck."

Caroline had broken into a sweat by the time she had made her way up the driveway and had reached the house. She considered turning back as she mounted the four stairs that led to the front door. Thank goodness for her cell phone. It was almost as if Polly was with her, sitting in her pocket, forcing her forward.

She reached out to ring the bell, almost unable to believe what she was about to do, when she remembered Polly's suggestion and folded her hand into a clenched fist. She rapped on the door three times. She had made it to the finish line. There was no turning back.

The door opened.

The woman standing before her in a cashmere sweater and jeans was Emily Kaplan. It was the girl who had been Caroline's first best friend, and in that moment, Caroline realized that Emily Kaplan had also been her best best friend. Not since that day in the cafeteria had Caroline had a friend as good as Emily. Not even close.

Her knees nearly buckled with the realization.

"Hello?" Emily said, and yes, it was Emily's voice as well. Emily's voice exactly. So little had changed about the woman. She looked older, of course, but not by much. And come to think of it, not older at all, really. Mature was more accurate. Emily looked like a more mature version of her teenage self, but still young and vital and strong.

"Hello?" Emily said again. Though she was smiling, Caroline could see that it wasn't real. A stranger had knocked on her door and was just staring at her. She was already nervous. "Can I help you?"

Caroline couldn't believe it. She had expected to confront her teenage nemesis, but had found her childhood friend instead.

"Is there something wrong, ma'am?" Emily asked, the smile that was not a smile fading into a look of consternation and fear. Caroline took a deep breath. She was trapped between the desire to run away and the impulse to embrace Emily as fiercely as she could.

"Mom!" Polly called out, sounding both frightened and annoyed. Caroline turned and saw Polly standing at the foot of the porch stairs, glaring up at her.

Caroline glared back, unable to find words even for Polly. Ten seconds had passed since Emily had opened the door, but it felt as if she had been standing in stunned silence for an eternity. For twenty-five years, in fact, which wasn't far from the truth.

"Miss? Maybe you should leave," Emily said.

Caroline turned back to her.

"I don't mean to be rude," Emily said. "But . . . I don't know. Is something wrong? Can I help? Does your mother need help?" Emily said, peeking around Caroline in order to make eye contact with Polly.

"Mom!" Polly said, shouting the word this time.

"Emily," Caroline said. "Emily, it's me. Caroline. Caroline Waters."

Recognition washed over Emily's face. "Caroline!" she said, exhaling the word as if she had been waiting an eon to say it. She reached out to embrace Caroline, and Caroline attempted to reciprocate but was unprepared for the speed and force of Emily's grip. Emily took Caroline's attempt at a polite hug and crushed it into her arms and chest as if she were hugging a paper doll. Caroline's well-formed defensive lines had been instantly overrun by Emily's unexpected emotion. She struggled to free one arm and then the other from Emily's embrace, then wrapped her arms around her childhood friend.

She couldn't believe how good it felt to be standing here, hugging a teary-eyed Emily Kaplan for the first time in forever.

"Fuck," Polly said, still standing at the bottom of the stairs, her voice not quite a whisper. "Fuck, fuck fuck."

fourteen

"What the hell are we doing in here?" Polly whispered between clenched teeth.

"I don't know," Caroline whispered back. "What was I supposed to do?" A second ago she was hugging the woman who she had despised for more than half of her life. Now she was sitting on the leather sofa in her living room, waiting for lemonade and cookies.

"Why did you say yes to lemonade?" Polly asked. "Say what you have to say so we can get out of here."

"It's not that simple."

"Yes, it is," Polly said. "Point your finger at her and tell her that she was a bitch and a bully in high school and that you hope she burns in hell. Then leave. It's not that hard."

Caroline sighed. "I'm not—"

"I hope you like oatmeal-raisin," Emily said, reentering the room. "It's all I have left."

"Great," Caroline said, thankful for the intrusion.

"I just ate," Polly said. "And Samuel Johnson thought oatmeal was best fed to horses."

Emily took a seat and slid tall glasses, complete with lemon wedges and sprigs of mint, over to Caroline and Polly. "Too bad for Samuel Johnson, then. More cookies for us."

Emily had become a woman who garnished lemonade with mint.

"I just can't believe that you're here," she said. "It's been so long. Have you been back to Blackstone since you left for college?"

"My mother still lives here," Caroline said. "So yes. But now that we're in Maryland, I don't get back very often."

"Mom doesn't like Blackstone," Polly said.

"That's not true," Caroline said. "I have some good memories from this place. It's just that I have some not-so-good memories, too. It's not always easy to come back."

"Of course," Emily said. "It must be so hard for you."

"Why did you name your house?" Polly asked.

"Oh, that was my husband's idea. He thinks that giving a house a name is a sign of respect for the work that went into it."

"What does the name mean?" Polly asked.

"It's an Aboriginal dialect. It means 'where the birds sing.'"

"You speak Aboriginal?" Polly asked.

"No," Emily said. "But Randy spent a semester in Australia and fell in love with the country."

"You have a lot of birds then?"

"Not really. It's more of a metaphor."

"A metaphor for what?"

"I don't know," Emily said. "A place where birds would want to sing."

"Maybe you should hang out some bird feeders," Polly said. "So the name would at least make some sense."

"Polly," Caroline said.

"It's okay," Emily said. "My daughter's the same way. Curious about everything."

"You have kids?" Caroline asked.

"Yes. Jake and Jane," Emily said, causing Polly to groan a little too loud. "Jake is twelve, and Jane is fifteen. She'll be home any minute. Jake is in middle school, so he gets home an hour later than Jane, which is nice. It gives us some time alone every afternoon when I'm not stuck at the shop. Girl time. You know?"

"Oh yeah," Polly said. "Mom and I are practically attached at the hip. Right, Mom?"

They were interrupted by the opening of the front door.

"Mom! I'm home!"

"In the living room," Emily called. "We have guests."

Jane Labonte was a tall, lanky girl with long, dark hair and a nose piercing that looked a lot like Polly's. She had a tattoo of an orange sun on her forearm and a black crescent moon on her neck. Her eye makeup was dark and her lips were a deep red. She was at least punk and possibly Goth in Caroline's estimation, except for the fact that she was smiling and had a bounce in her step. Here was a girl who exuded happiness.

"How was school?" Emily asked.

"Great," Jane said, and then extended her hand to Caroline and Polly. "Hi. I'm Jane."

"Hi, I'm Caroline. I'm one of your mother's friends from high school. This is Polly."

Polly didn't move.

"Oh wow!" Jane said. "You knew my mom in high school?"

"I think they were a lot friendlier before high school," Polly said. "Isn't that right, Mom?"

"Um, yes. Your mom and I lived next door to each other until high school. Then my family moved."

"Oh, you're Caroline Waters!" Jane said, eyes widening. "Mom talks about you all the time!"

"She does?" Caroline said.

"You do?" Polly said.

"Of course," Emily said. "Caroline, you were my best friend growing up. I hated the fact that we drifted apart after you moved. I've probably told Randy a thousand times that I wished you and I could get back together. I had hoped that you would come for a reunion, but you never showed. Then I tried finding you on Facebook but couldn't."

"Mom doesn't believe in Facebook. Even my nana's on Facebook."

Jane laughed.

"Why don't you take Polly down the street to The Spot, so Caroline and I can catch up. If you have the time, Caroline?"

"The Spot?"

"It's a little hamburger place that opened up across the street from the high school. The kids get soda and ice cream there after school. It's made up like a 1950s diner. Probably to reassure parents that nothing bad is happening inside."

"Nothing bad *is* happening," Jane said.

"Take a twenty out of my purse and take Polly," Emily said. "Maybe get a soda if you guys aren't hungry."

"Sure," Jane said.

Polly turned to her mother. There was pleading in her eyes but also resignation and perhaps a hint of scolding. Caroline guessed that they said something like *The last thing I want to do is drink a soda with this girl, but I'll do my part as long as you do your part and say what needs to be said.*

"Go ahead," Caroline said. "Just be back in an hour or so. We can't be late for Nana." Caroline wanted to establish an escape plan and hoped Polly would go along with it. The girls walked out the front door, leaving Caroline and Emily alone.

"Let's sit out back," Emily said. "Wait till you see the view."

The view from the elevated deck, complete with Adirondack chairs, was of the high school and the pond just beyond it. The school looked exactly as Caroline remembered it. A sprawling, two-story, red-brick structure surrounded by asphalt parking lots, open fields, and an adjacent cinder track. Caroline could see Polly and Jane walking down the hill toward the school; she was surprised to see them engaged in what appeared to be an animated conversation.

"So fill me in on the last twenty-five years," Caroline said. This was a strategy she had adopted long ago—one she imagined many shy people used. Ask a lot of questions. Keep the other person talking.

And she needed Emily to talk. Despite the warm greeting, Caroline's plan was still to deliver the comeback she should have delivered years ago. Not that she knew what that would be, exactly.

And there was something else.

It wasn't the warm embrace or the revelation that Emily had attempted to reconnect with Caroline that was holding her back. There was a shadow lingering behind Emily's eyes. Something was wrong. Caroline was certain of it. Emily Kaplan-turned-Labonte might be pushing forty, but those were the same eyes of the girl who had once fallen out of the birch tree in her backyard and broken her leg. There had been pain in her eyes that day, but that pain had been nothing compared to what she could see behind Emily's eyes now.

That didn't matter, Caroline told herself. She had come here to say something important, and regardless of what Emily might be going through, it needed to be said. Polly was right. Emily would either deny the charges completely or pass off the incident as a transgression of youth. It would probably become an amusing story for her to tell at dinner parties: *The time this girl from high school came back to town to tell me I was a bitch because of something I can't even remember doing.*

But for Caroline, it would mean something. It would mean that the pregnant pause, one that had lasted nearly a quarter of a century, would finally come to an end. She felt as if she had been holding her breath since that day, that in some sad way she was still standing by the empty table, still searching for the right words that would return her best best friend to her side.

Now she had those words. They would not bring Emily and Caroline back together, but they would allow Caroline to breathe again. To step away from that empty cafeteria table and resume her life in the direction it should have been headed all along.

This was Caroline's moment.

Emily was describing the four years that she and Randy spent together at Boston College, then the three years that they had spent completing their graduate degrees: she at Northeastern, he at Harvard. With school behind them, they returned to Blackstone, bought a home on Elm Street, and started their family. Randy joined a psychiatric practice in Newton, and about five years ago left to start his own practice with offices in Milford and Providence. Emily had never put her English degree "to any use" (the air quotes were Emily's), but when Jake entered high school in three years, she was planning on looking for work in advertising or corporate communications.

Caroline was about to ask what a person in corporate communications did when she saw something out of the corner of her eye. She turned to see a man, a tall, middle-aged man walking quickly across the living room and toward the deck. "Hello," he said as his approached. "I don't think we've met."

"Randy," Emily said, rising from her seat. "I didn't know you'd be home early."

Caroline hadn't seen it at first, but after hearing Emily say his name, she could see the ghost of Randy Labonte in the red-faced man still coming toward them. He hadn't aged nearly as well as his wife. His hairline had receded dramatically. His face was fuller. Fatter. Almost a second chin. There were wrinkles around his eyes. He wasn't fat, but he was nothing like the athlete that Caroline remembered.

"Surprise, surprise," he said, and though he smiled, the words sounded like they came with a sneer. Something was wrong.

"Hi," Caroline said, rising to her feet. "I'm Caroline Jacobs. Waters. You'd remember me as Caroline Waters."

"Who?"

"I went to school with you. Caroline Waters. Emily and I were friends when we were little."

Randy turned to Emily. "I didn't know you were reconnecting with high school friends," Randy said. That edge to his voice. He sounded angry. He didn't look angry. But he was angry. No doubt about it.

He turned back to Caroline, his face still red with anger. "Caroline Waters, you said?"

"You don't remember me. I was quiet back then. It's okay."

"Caroline just stopped by for a visit," Emily said. "It was a surprise."

"A surprise visit, huh?" Randy looked from Caroline to Emily. "You don't see those much these days."

"Actually, you and I had chemistry together," Caroline said. "Mrs. Murphy's class. I sat in front of you. Remember?"

"Caroline came up from Maryland yesterday," Emily explained. "She happened to be in town and decided to stop by and take a chance on my being home."

"Yeah, I came from Maryland," Caroline said, feeling the need to support Emily but not sure why.

"You came all the way from Maryland just to drop by and see Emily?" He turned to his wife. "That's ridiculous."

Emily's eyes flashed from Randy to Caroline then back to Randy. She was trying to make a decision, Caroline thought. Trying to decide how much to say. After two days of half-truths and partial stories told to her daughter and husband, Caroline understood the problem well.

"Why don't I leave you guys alone?" she said. "I can come back another time." She saw Emily's eyes widen at the mention of her leaving.

"No," she said. "Please don't go." She turned to Randy. "Fine. There never was a 'friend.' Okay? I did it all by myself."

"What?" Randy's anger melted into momentary confusion.

"I told you that I was talking to a girlfriend because I didn't want you to think that I was crazy. I didn't want you to think that I was the only one who thought that you and Cara were bad for us."

"What about reading the texts?" Randy asked. "The cell phone tracking?"

"I did that myself. Anyone can do it. Just go to the Web site and you'll see. It wasn't rocket science. It's actually an option offered by the phone company."

"You're telling me that your so-called friend of yours was fake? And her husband and all her agreeable friends were fake, too?"

"I should probably be going," Caroline said.

"I was too embarrassed to tell anyone what you were doing, but I couldn't stand being all alone. I wanted you to know how wrong people would see it if they only knew."

"That's fucked up," Randy said. "I don't believe it."

"I don't care if you believe it or not. It's the truth."

"You expect me to believe that . . . ," he said, waving a finger in Caroline's direction.

"Caroline," Caroline said. "Caroline Jacobs."

"You expect me to believe that Caroline has nothing to do with this. She just stopped by for a visit. That she doesn't know anything about me and Cara."

"I don't," Caroline interjected. "I actually have no idea what you guys are talking about."

Randy looked from Emily to Caroline and then back to Emily. "I don't know what to believe. Either you've been lying to me all along, or you're lying to me now. I don't know which is worse." He turned to Caroline. "Look, if you're really not involved with this, I'm sorry. I'm really sorry. Finish your visit. If that's what this is."

Randy turned. It was an angry, dramatic turn, the kind that you only see on television and in movies, and apparently for good reason. As he turned, his foot caught in the floor rug and he lost his balance. He tripped. He raised his hands to brace himself for the fall, and as he did, his open palms struck the sliding glass door. Cracks fired out from the two spots where his hands connected with the glass, spider-webbing toward the frame. A second later, it gave way, breaking into large pieces, sending Randy through the window and onto the deck in a sprawl.

fifteen

Caroline moved first, closing the gap and reaching Randy, who had rolled onto his back after striking the ground. He was holding his hands above him and swearing, a constant stream of panicked, angry expletives. Both hands were bleeding, but Caroline could tell at once that the wounds were not serious. Blood was trickling down his bare arms, not streaming.

A flesh wound, Polly would say in an English accent, though Caroline still didn't understand the reference.

"Don't move," Caroline said. "Let me see your hands." Caroline examined each one, looking to see if there was any glass embedded in the skin. She saw none. She turned and saw Emily, still frozen in her spot by her chair, surveying the scene with wide eyes and white knuckles, too shocked to move.

"Help me lift him up," Caroline said, feeling oddly in charge despite the circumstances. "I don't want him to cut his elbows or knees on the glass."

Caroline took one hand and Emily took the other, and together, they pulled Randy up and out of the pile of broken glass.

"Should I call an ambulance?" Emily asked.

"I don't think we need one," Caroline said. "Go run your hands under the kitchen sink. As long as there isn't any glass jammed too far into the skin, I think you'll be okay. You got lucky. If that glass had broken when you first fell into it, I think it would've been much worse."

"Okay," Randy said, staring down at his hands. All his anger and indignation was gone. It was as if the universe had chastised him for his behavior. He headed for the kitchen.

"I'll help," Emily said, turning to follow her husband. Then she stopped and looked back. "Listen, Caroline. I can't . . . I mean, could you . . ."

"Get him bandaged up. Just point me to a broom and dustpan so I can sweep this up. Then we can talk. Or not. Whatever you want."

Emily smiled a little. "Okay," she said. "Thanks."

"You don't have to say a thing," Caroline said, when Emily returned to the living room some fifteen minutes later. "It's none of my business." She had decided upon these two sentences while sweeping up the glass. A small part of her still wanted to complete her original mission and hurt this woman, but Caroline couldn't bring herself to humiliate her any more than she already had been. Caroline had entered the home of her high school nemesis, the mean girl who had changed the course of her life in ways she was just beginning to understand. But now, more than ever, that girl also seemed like the childhood friend she had once loved.

"He's got this friend at work," Emily said. "Cara. He says it's nothing. Just a friend. It's probably true. A man can have a woman for a friend. Right? I just don't know if that's what this is. I think maybe it's not."

"You don't need to tell me this."

"That's the problem," Emily said. "I haven't told anyone."

"But Randy seemed to think—"

"I didn't want to tell any of my friends. It's too embarrassing. And it might be nothing. And if it's nothing, I don't want my girlfriends to hate him forever. They all think he's so sweet. But I didn't want to be the crazy, jealous wife so I told him that I've been talking to one of my friends about it. I just wouldn't tell him which friend."

"Have you met this woman yet? Do you know her?"

Emily opened her mouth to answer, and her expression transformed from anger to sadness. Her eyes welled with tears and her bottom lip quivered in a way that Caroline remembered from their childhood.

"It's okay," Caroline said. "We don't have to talk about any of this. I can go."

"No it's not okay," she said. "They work together all day. He sees her more than me. Then when they're not together, they're texting each other. All the time. Nights. Weekends. I don't care what he says. It's just not right." She began to cry.

Caroline put her arm around her friend and pulled her close. Emily sobbed for a solid minute until, with great resolve, she took a few deep breaths, straightened her back, and wiped her face with her palms. "The girls will be back soon," she said. "I don't want Jane to see me like this. The kids don't know."

"Okay," Caroline said.

Emily sighed. "I haven't told anyone about it. You're the only one. It's just so humiliating."

"Is Randy okay?" Caroline asked.

"No, he's not okay," Emily said. "He's texting some girl ten years younger than me a hundred times a day. We have kids, for Christ's sake. What the hell is he thinking?"

"No, I mean his hands. Are his hands okay?"

Emily smiled a little. "Sorry. Yes, they're fine."

"You have some blood on your shirt," she said, pointing to Emily's blouse. "And your pants, too."

"Damn it. I'd better change."

As Emily stood to leave the room, Randy reentered. He offered Caroline a sheepish smile. "I'm fine. Just a couple small cuts. Thanks for the help."

"I told her the truth," Emily said.

Caroline wished she could slink beneath the couch cushions and disappear.

"I got blood on my shirt," Emily said. "I have to change."

"Okay," Randy said.

Randy waited until Emily had left the room before sitting down in a chair opposite Caroline. "I'm sorry about this," he said. "Not exactly what you expected when you decided to pay your childhood friend a visit."

"You believe me, then," Caroline said.

"Yes. I actually remember you now. If I had taken half a second to use my brain, I would've recognized you. It's just—it's been a tough few weeks. And I can be an idiot sometimes."

"It's all right. I'm just glad you're okay."

"Thanks," he said, taking a seat in a chair opposite her. "So tell me, why are you back in Blackstone? Is your family still here?

"My mom still lives here," Caroline said, feeling more uncomfortable by the moment. She had come with the intention of destroying a woman and now she felt as if she was betraying her by talking to her possibly unfaithful husband. "Maybe I should go," Caroline said. "The girls are probably on their way back. I could pick up Polly and drive Jane home if you'd like."

"No, I should go," Randy said. "You and Emily haven't seen each other in years. Don't let me ruin your visit any more than I already have."

"It's fine. I think you and Emily have more important things to talk about anyway."

"I think we're all talked out, to be honest."

At that moment, the front door opened. Jane and Polly entered, sipping sodas.

"We're back!" Jane said.

"Hi, Mom," Polly said, sounding a little too normal for Caroline's liking.

Caroline took the opportunity to stand, hoping to use this change in position as the momentum she needed to affect a graceful exit. "Hi, girls," she said. "Did you have a good time?"

"We did," Polly said. "It was loads of fun."

Now Caroline knew that something was up.

"Yeah, we had a good time," Jane said. "Hey, Mom, what are we doing for dinner tonight?"

"I hadn't thought about it yet," Emily said. She had reentered the room. Caroline wondered how long she had been standing there.

"Perfect," Jane said. "Polly's grandmother invited us over for dinner. You knew her when you were a kid, too. Right?"

"I did," Emily said. "But I haven't seen her in years."

"That's why my nana invited you to dinner," Polly explained. "She wants to see you. Catch up on old times."

"Catch up on old times?" Caroline said, more to herself than anyone in the room.

"She's the lady who owns the pet cemetery," Jane added. "The one on Main Street. I've always wanted to see it, but Dad made me bury Mr. Wiggins in the woods. Remember?"

"I remember," Emily said, turning to Caroline. "I didn't know that was your mother."

"Nana invited Emily and Jane over for dinner?" Caroline asked. She couldn't imagine a scenario in which her mother would do such a thing.

"Jane's dad and brother, too," Polly added. "The whole family."

At his mention, Randy Labonte rose. "Hi, I'm Randy," he said, holding his hand out to Polly. "Mr. Labonte, I guess, to you."

"Hi, I'm Polly. Nice to meet you, Mr. Labonte. Can you come for dinner, too?" she asked.

"I don't see why not," Randy said.

"What happened to the door?" Jane asked, pointing in that direction.

"A little accident," Emily said.

"Everythink okay?" Jane asked warily.

"A-okay, muffin," Emily said. "Everything's fine. Just fine."

"Nana really invited Emily and her family over for dinner?" Caroline said.

"Yes," Polly said, sounding annoyed. "Six o'clock. Barbecued chicken. It's going to be a blast. Nothing better than sharing a meal with old friends and new friends. Right, Mom?"

Now Caroline knew that something was up.

sixteen

As soon as they were back in the car and moving, Polly removed her phone from her pocket.

"Don't you want to know how it went?" Caroline asked.

She planned on lying to Polly. She would tell her that harsh words had been exchanged, an apology had been offered, and it was now all water under the bridge. She had no desire to share Emily and Randy Labonte's marital struggles with her daughter, nor did she want to be chastised by Polly for failing in her mission.

"Hi, Nana," Polly said, her face pressed against the phone. "I hope you don't mind, but I invited Mom's friend Emily and her family over for dinner tonight."

"She doesn't know?" Caroline said.

"Yeah. Can you make barbecued chicken?" A pause, and then Polly said, "Exactly." Another pause and then, "I'll let her tell you. Thanks, Nana. I'll see you soon. Bye!"

"You invited them for dinner?" Caroline said. "What were you thinking?"

"I was thinking that after those oatmeal-raisin cookies, there was no way you were going to tell Emily off. If I didn't force the two of you together again, it might never happen."

Caroline pulled the car over to the side of the road, skidding to a halt on the gravel shoulder. "You had no right to do that."

"I had every right," Polly said. "Isn't that the whole reason you dragged me here in the first place?"

"Inviting Emily over for dinner was not your job. Lying to me was not your job."

"Well, maybe if you had done your job, I wouldn't have had to do mine."

"It's not that simple," Caroline said.

"Yes, it is. I'm not saying it's easy, but it is simple. You just have to speak up for once in your life."

That hit Caroline like a spear through the heart.

"I know you were trying to help, and I know I asked for your help, but it's never okay to lie. It wasn't fair to me or Emily or Nana."

"Give me a break," Polly said.

"What?"

"For a second there, I thought we were going to have an actual conversation. But then you switched right back into bullshit mode."

"That's not bullshit mode," Caroline said. "It's responsible mode. It's parent mode."

"No, Mom, it's bullshit mode. You don't have a parent mode. You have hide-under-a-rock mode and pray-things-get-better mode, but you don't have anything close to parent mode. Just because you're my mom doesn't mean we can't have an actual conversation about real things, except you can never do that."

"Are you kidding me? Every time I try to talk to you, you push me away. Or walk away."

"That's because you never have anything to say. It's like you're on some loser TV show pretending to be a mom instead just being an actual person. These past two days have been the most real I've ever seen you in my life. I was pissed at you for letting Grace Dinali ambush me in chemistry, but at least you stood up to her mother. It was like the first time you ever went off script."

"You're my daughter," Caroline said. "Not my friend."

"No, because you don't have any friends. You have Wendy, who lives on the other side of the country, and that's it. No wonder why that bitch kicked you out of her table."

"I can't believe you would throw that back at me." Caroline's voice was trembling.

"Whatever," Polly said, and threw open the car door.

"What are you doing?"

"Walking away. Like you said I do." Polly slammed the car door and started walking down the hill back in the direction of the high school.

Caroline opened the door and stepped out onto the gravel. "You're going to walk all the way back to Grandma's house?"

"I know the way," Polly said, not bothering to look back.

"Polly, it's like five miles away. Get back in the car."

Polly said nothing. A second later, she pressed her phone against her ear and began talking.

Caroline waited another minute and then climbed back into the car. She watched as Polly crested the top of a gentle slope and then disappeared like the setting sun. When she could no longer see her daughter, she turned the car around and headed in the opposite direction.

Caroline did not intentionally drive to the intersection of Summer and Federal streets, but she found herself there just the same.

It took less than five minutes.

Heading south on Summer Street past a long line of nearly identical split-level homes, Caroline pulled the car alongside the road, coming to a stop on a grassy shoulder fifty feet from where the two roads met. Summer and Federal streets joined at a three-way intersection, with Federal connecting to Summer at a not quite ninety-degree angle. Drivers heading south (in the direction that Caroline was now facing) would have to make a hard right turn onto Federal. But if they were traveling north on Summer, they would be able to make a more gradual turn, bearing left onto Federal unless there was oncoming traffic, which was exactly what Caroline had been doing on her bike that day so long ago.

She and Lucy had been pedaling north, hoping to arrive home in time for lunch. Caroline was maybe fifty feet ahead of her younger sister, who had fallen behind on the last hill. As she approached the turn onto Federal Street, she peered over her shoulder to check for oncoming traffic. She saw Lucy, her Laura Ingalls braids bobbing in rhythm as she stood atop her pedals, pumping hard to catch up with her big sister. Her cheeks were flushed, her face was streaked with sweat, but she was smiling as she caught Caroline's eye. She was happy. She was coming to the end of an adventure with her big sister.

Caroline saw the yellow van cresting the far hill, a golden speck on the horizon. Plenty of time to bear left onto Federal Street before the van caught up to her, and so she did, twisting her handlebars and leaning into the turn.

She was pedaling up a slight incline when she heard the thump and then the screech of tires, in that order. Thump then screech. An order that would come to mean so much to policemen and lawyers and a stranger who would be a stranger no longer.

Investigators would later say that Lucy had probably not seen the yellow van, which would eventually become *the speeding yellow van,* when she crossed over to Federal Street. It might have been in her blind spot. Or more likely, she had simply misjudged the van's high speed. Lucy had probably looked over her shoulder, gauged the distance, determined that she had plenty of time to cross, not realizing how quickly the van was devouring the pavement between them.

But Caroline knew that Lucy had never taken the time to look over her shoulder to check for traffic. She had seen Caroline cross over onto Federal Street, and ten seconds later, she had followed, assuming that her big sister was looking out for her, as she had so often.

Caroline looked and Caroline crossed so now I can cross.

The van broadsided her, launching the pink Schwinn forward like a rocket. A second later, the screech, as the driver of the vehicle, a twenty-four-year-old woman named Katherine Paley, slammed on the brakes in a vain attempt to stop the van from running over the girl. The doctors would later say that it didn't matter. Lucy was dead before she even hit the pavement. Her head had struck the front of the van with such force that she had died instantly. Painlessly. Probably unaware of what had even happened. Caroline wondered if this is what all doctors said about dead little girls in order to ease the family's pain.

Caroline turned in time to see Lucy's body tumbling beneath the skidding van like a doll flopping around inside a dryer.

The first scream had not been her own but that of Katherine Paley. Caroline could see the woman now, more than two decades later, still clear as day. Faded blue jeans. Purple sweater. Blond hair hanging past narrow shoulders. Sneakered feet straddling the double yellow line of Summer Street. Hands latched on to her temples as she screamed a scream that Caroline could hear to this day.

Then her gaze shifted from the spot where Katherine Paley had been standing to the spot in the road where Lucy's body had finally come to rest. Caroline knew that particular spot on the pavement better than any place in the world, even though she was still unable to recall the last time she had been here. That tiny patch of cracked asphalt had become the center of Caroline's universe. Everything that she had seen and done and said since that day had spun out from that tiny spot.

Now she could see the fifteen-year-old version of herself, dropping her bike in the middle of the road and racing over to her sister, her screams mingling with those of Katherine Paley's to fill the air with high-pitched hysterics. Caroline had known that her sister was dead before she even reached the body. She remembered the sense of her stomach dropping out from underneath her, the sudden loss of balance, then skidding, falling, collapsing onto the pavement ten feet before reaching her sister. The first heave of breath that her lungs demanded and then the agonizing, weeping crawl across the pavement, over the double yellow line, until she finally reached Lucy's lifeless body. She had wanted to grab her sister and hold on to her, not let anyone touch her. She wanted so desperately to believe that as long as Lucy remained untouched by the world, the world could not take her. And at the same time she wanted to fix her sister, twist her arm back where it belonged, turn her head so that body and neck and face were properly lined up once again. She fell atop Lucy's body, grabbed all that she could and wept, knowing that her sister was dead and that is was her fault. Would always be her fault.

And she was weeping again now, staring at that spot in the road where she had last held her baby sister. Tears streaked her cheeks and mucus filled her nose as she whispered "I'm sorry" over and over again. A lifetime of apologies that could never make up for that ugly moment on that perfect autumn day.

As she wept, her eyes shifted from the spot on the pavement where her sister had lain to the patch of pavement on Federal Street where she had dropped her bike. She could see that, too, now, a Huffy ten-speed, metallic blue, its front tire spinning silently, the white and red plastic bag still hanging from its handlebars. The bag would not enter her thoughts until later, once her bike had found its way home, returned by the police during those fuzzy hours after the accident. Caroline had disposed of it before any-one had time to question its existence, which was to say that she placed the bag and its contents in the spot where her mother was least likely to look. And she had been right. As far as Caroline knew, it was still sitting there today. She had hidden the bag from the police and her mother for more than two decades, but more important, she had hidden the bag from herself.

seventeen

Caroline was surprised to see two cars parked beside her mother's. One was George Durrow's minivan; she had never seen the other before. Mr. Durrow was sitting on the front porch in one of her mother's oversized rocking chairs. Sitting beside him in an identical rocker was an older man, thin, bald and wearing a pair of large, dark sunglasses. They were drinking lemonade from tall glasses.

"It's Caroline? Right?" Durrow asked as Caroline mounted the porch steps. He had changed clothes. He was now wearing dress pants and a sweater, with a paisley tie peaking above the collar.

"Yes, it is," she said. "You're Mr. Durrow. Right?"

"Call me George."

"All right," she said. "George, then."

"And I'm Spartacus," the other man said, grinning.

"Spartacus?" Caroline repeated. She reached out to shake the man's hand, but he offered none in return. She reached a little closer, thinking that perhaps he was older and less mobile than he appeared. Nothing.

"You're trying to shake my hand," the man said, smirking. "Aren't you?"

"Excuse me?" Caroline said.

"I'm blind," he said, seeming to hone in on her voice. "I'm sorry. I thought you knew."

"Oh God, I'm sorry," Caroline said. "I had no idea."

"Nor should you," he said, extending his hand in her general direction.

"It's nice to meet you," she said. "You are?"

"I told you. I am Spartacus." When Caroline failed to respond, he added, "For real."

"Spartacus? Like from the movie?"

"That's his name," George Durrow said. "I didn't believe it either when he first told me."

"I don't believe it. Show me your driver's license."

Spartacus laughed.

"Oh, I'm sorry," Caroline said.

"I think it's rude that the state won't let me drive just because I can't see, but that's my lot in life. A least until Google gets those self-driving cars on the road. Did you know that in Iowa, a blind man can get a gun permit? Now that's a progressive state. But ask your mother. The name is real."

"I'm really sorry," Caroline said.

"Don't worry about it," Spartacus said. "You're certainly not the first to question me. I was supposed to be an Edwin, but when I was born blind, my parents decided to go with Spartacus. They thought I needed all the help I could get. And they were hippies, so it wasn't much of a stretch."

Caroline smiled.

"I love it," George said. "Hippies or not, it was smart of them."

"And your last name?" Caroline said. "Dare I ask?"

"Bloom," Spartacus said. "Doesn't quite match the first, but there was no changing that."

"Your parents sound like a couple of interesting characters," Caroline said.

"They were," Spartacus said. "They're not with us anymore."

"I'm sorry. I'm saying all the wrong things today."

"Don't be ridiculous," Spartacus said. "I miss them dearly, but there's nothing to be sorry about. Even Kirk Douglas will die someday."

"Kirk Douglas?" Caroline asked.

"The actor who played Spartacus."

"Right," Caroline said, relieved that this banter had turned her mood around. She was surprised, too. Small talk was not her forte, yet she felt at ease with these two men, even with all of her gaffs. She pulled up a chair. "So you're here for the same reason as George?" she asked.

"I hope not!" Spartacus said. "Is there something you want to tell me, George?"

George laughed uncomfortably. "Penelope's a fine lady," George said. "But I wouldn't dream of stealing her."

"Stealing?" Caroline said.

"You didn't know that your mother was dating?" Spartacus asked.

"No, I knew she was dating," Caroline said. "I just didn't know—"

"That her boyfriend was blind?"

"No," Caroline said. "That his name was Spartacus." Another smile.

"That's your mother. She loves the shock value. When we first started dating, she'd have me meet her friends at lunch on some outdoor patio so my sunglasses didn't look so out of the ordinary. And she'd make sure that we arrived before her friends, so they wouldn't see my cane or see me walking in on her arm. Then she'd just wait until one of them was brave enough to ask if I was blind."

"And you went along with it?" Caroline asked.

"Sure," Spartacus said. "I have to admit that it made for an interesting sociological experiment."

"Sounds cruel to me," George said.

"Sounds like my mother to me," Caroline said.

"I can't deny that it had Penelope written all over it," Spartacus said. "She enjoyed screwing with people so much that I started to wonder if it was the only reason she agreed to date me."

"That's Mom," Caroline said.

"Good thing I love her." Spartacus Bloom loved her mother. This made Caroline surprisingly happy. It also made her wonder how much she was missing out on. "By the way," she said, "have you seen my daughter?"

"She got here an hour ago," George said.

"Really? She must've run. She was over by the high school when I last saw her."

"No," George said, "She came with . . . I can't remember their names."

"She wasn't walking?"

"No, she was in that SUV over there," George said, pointing to the Lexus. "A family. Husband, wife, two kids."

"Really?" Caroline said.

"The fella had bandages on his hands."

"The Labontes?" Caroline asked. "Emily and Randy Labonte?"

"Yup, that's them."

"They're here now?" Caroline felt a weight descend upon her chest.

"Yeah, they've been here almost as long as I have," George said. "It was nice of Polly to invite me, by the way. That's quite a girl you have."

"Oh, you're here for dinner, too?"

"Yeah," Mr. Durrow said. "I hope you don't mind."

"She invited me, too," Spartacus said. "Penelope told me to stay away tonight. She said she wanted dinner with her girls. But then Polly called and told me to come right over, so here I am. Hope it's all right."

"Of course it is," Caroline said. "The more the merrier. Right?"

And why should she mind? This promised to be a great evening. Her mother's blind boyfriend, a parrot-grieving client, her high school nemesis, her nemesis's possibly adulterous husband, and their daughter. Plus a son Caroline had yet to meet. A perfect combination for a dinner party.

As if reading her thoughts, Spartacus said, "Agnes is here, too."

"Agnes?" Caroline asked.

"My home health aide," Spartacus said. "She drove me here, and Polly invited her to stay. It's going to be one hell of a dinner party."

That was exactly what Caroline was afraid of.

eighteen

It was possible that Polly was acting out of kindness and a spirit of hospitality, but Caroline didn't think so. Her daughter was not the kind of girl to arrange a dinner party for even her closest friends. And she was never one to enjoy the company of strangers.

Like it or not, she had to admit that Polly was doing exactly what she had been told to do. Caroline had pointed her daughter at a target and told her not to veer off course no matter what she might say. She was doing exactly that.

It had seemed like a good plan in the confines of the car and even in the New Jersey diner, but now that it was being put into practice, well, the truth was that Polly was scaring the hell out of her. Her daughter had proven herself to be more than capable of bending the world to her will, and Caroline had given her license to do so.

Caroline was six steps into the house when she ran into Randy Labonte—literally—causing him to spill red wine across the front of his sweater.

"Oh, God. I'm so sorry," she said.

"Don't be silly," Randy said, reaching into a bathroom for a hand towel. "Just a case of two objects reaching the same point in space at the same time."

"You're a mess," Caroline said, taking the towel and dabbing his sweater.

"More than you know," Randy said.

"I'm not making any progress here," she said, still dabbing. "Follow me. We need to get it into the wash before the stain sets in." She led Randy back down the hallway and through the basement door. At the bottom of the stairs, Caroline flipped a switch, brightening the darkened space. A washer and dryer were tucked away in a corner near the stairs. She led Randy over to them.

"You have a shirt on under that, I assume?" Caroline said.

"Yes," Randy said, pulling his sweater over his head. Caroline laughed as she realized that this was the second time in the past two hours that she had watched this man ruin a shirt.

"What?" he said.

"You're going through shirts left and right today. Aren't you?"

"I guess I am."

Caroline applied stain remover to the sweater and tossed it into the ancient appliance.

"What's all this?" Randy asked, stepping farther into the basement. Spread throughout the dimly lit space were large pieces of furniture covered by thick sheets of plastic. Sofas, armchairs, a dining room table, and a bedroom set along with smaller items— brass candlesticks, a bowling ball, an empty picture frame.

"When we moved from our old house," Caroline said, "we had to downsize, so Mom moved all the furniture into the basement. All this was supposed to be temporary. She was planning on having a yard sale, but when my sister died, Mom stopped throwing things away. So everything's just sat down here ever since."

"She can't let it go?" Randy said, tracing his finger through the dust on a sheet of plastic.

"I guess not. She hasn't touched Lucy's bedroom, either. It's sort of a shrine to her now."

"It must be hard to move on when you lose a child," Randy said. "I can't begin to even imagine. I remember hearing about your sister when it happened, but I didn't really know her all that well. I guess I didn't know you all that well, either."

Caroline turned the dial on the washing machine and pressed

START. "Yeah, we didn't really travel in the same circles in high school."

"It's odd," he said, "because you and Emily were so close for so long. It's a shame how people sometimes drift apart."

How could he not know? He had to know.

"Your mom seems to be doing well now," Randy said, moving deeper into the basement, as if to inspect every piece of furniture through its milky, plastic sheath.

"It was a long time before she was normal again," Caroline said. She walked towards the stairs, hoping Randy would follow. She didn't like it down here. Too many memories. "But if all she's got to show for what she went through is a basement full of old furniture that she can't let go of, I'd say she's doing pretty good."

Randy stopped beside the bed that her mother and father had shared so long ago. He turned back to her. "And now she runs a pet cemetery and deals with death all the time. Kind of ironic, huh?"

"Not really," Caroline said. "Mom went from not handling death well at all to becoming an expert on it. Kind of like those people who convert to a new religion. They sometimes become more religious than the people who were born into the religion. Same thing with Mom."

"I guess she decided to own it," Randy said.

"Exactly."

Randy bent down to get a better look at the console television that once dominated their home on Farm Street. "How old were you when your father split?"

"Fifteen," she said. "Same age as my daughter, actually."

"Jane, too," Randy said.

"Yeah? She seems great. I haven't met your son yet."

"Jake. He's twelve. A good kid. A smart-ass, but I think most kids are at his age."

"Polly certainly is," Caroline said.

"It must've been hard to lose your father at that age."

"Yeah," Caroline said. "When he left, I sort of lost my mother, too. I never really got her back."

"What do you mean?"

"That woman upstairs isn't the one I grew up with. It's weird. She's kind of like a stranger to me. I think Polly knows her better than I do. When I left for college, she was a mess. Depressed. Drinking. While I was gone, she completely transformed herself. I think I'm a little jealous, to be honest. I could never pull off something like that."

"What happened to your father?" Randy asked. "Do you still see him?

"No. He moved to Florida and never came back. He sent money every now and then, but that was it."

Randy stepped over to an armchair in the far corner. He pulled back the plastic and ran his hand along an upholstered arm.

"That was my father's chair," Caroline said. "He used to read to me in that chair when I was little. It's so strange how a man goes from loving his children so much to just leaving them behind."

"I'm not cheating on Emily, if that's what she told you."

"Emily didn't tell me anything. And it's really none of my business."

"I haven't done anything wrong."

"It's really none of my business," Caroline repeated. "We should head back upstairs. I'll come back for your sweater after dinner." She took a couple steps in the direction of the staircase, hoping again that her momentum would pull him along.

Randy sighed. "I've been with Emily since we were seventeen. She's only the third girl I ever kissed. I'd never really flirted with a girl before Emily. I never even flirted with Emily. She asked me out, and I said yes. That was it."

"You have a wife and kids. We don't get to do everything we want in life. Sometimes we have to leave things behind."

"Easier said than done," he said.

"Not when you have a wife and kids," Caroline said. "Kids should make things pretty clear. At least it did for me."

"Are we supposed to give up on our dreams when we get married?"

"If flirting with girls is your dream, you need to rethink your priorities."

They stood in silence for a moment, a couch and a coffee table wrapped in plastic separating them. Caroline hadn't noticed, but her hands were balled into fists. She was angry. This man was a little boy, and she found herself feeling sorry for Emily because of it. "I don't think my mother even knows I'm here. I'd better get upstairs and see if she needs some help."

She reemerged from the basement into a house of hustle and bustle. A thin, young woman who Caroline didn't recognize was passing through the hallway into the dining room carrying a large bowl of potato salad. She could hear conversations coming from the kitchen and the living room.

She found her mother and Polly in the kitchen. Her mother was pulling a pan of chicken from the oven. Polly was filling a glass pitcher with water from the tap.

"It's about time you showed your face," her mother said. "Polly's turned my peaceful evening in front of the television into a full-blown party. What was she thinking?"

"I've been asking myself the same question," Caroline said, glancing over at Polly. Polly avoided eye contact, turning quickly in the direction of the dining room with two pitchers of ice water in her hands.

"What's she up to?" Caroline asked.

"What do you mean?"

"Why the sudden need to invite everyone she knows to your house for dinner?"

"What are you talking about?" her mother asked. "She barely knows any of them."

"Exactly. Emily's family, your boyfriend, who you never told me was blind by the way, and George Durrow. That's a strange guest list."

"Agnes, too," her mother added. "Spartacus's aide. I hate that girl."

"This doesn't strike you as a little odd?"

"I don't know. I think it's going to be fun. I can't remember the last time I had this many people for dinner. So you met Spartacus, then?"

"Yeah. Why didn't you tell me that he's blind? Or that his name is Spartacus?"

"I don't know. I guess I didn't think it's his most important quality."

"Okay, Mom. Sure."

Polly reappeared in the kitchen. "I think we're all set. Should I put out that chicken, too?"

"No, there should be plenty on the table. I'll leave this here to cool in case we need more."

"Polly," Caroline said, motioning her to stop. "What's going on?"

"Dinner. Can't you tell?"

"I'm serious. What are you doing?"

"I thought it would be nice for you to have dinner with Emily, and I wasn't going to invite her over alone. Can you give me a break? I'm just trying to do the right thing. Okay?"

It wasn't okay, and Caroline knew it.

"Caroline," her mother said. "Go get Spartacus and George from the porch, and then sit down."

Caroline obeyed her mother's instructions, escorting the men through the house and to the dining room. Two extra leaves had been added to the table, making it longer than Caroline had ever seen it. The woman with the potato salad was Agnes, who was much younger than her name implied. She rose upon seeing Spartacus enter the room and guided him to a seat beside her. Caroline could see why her mother didn't like this woman. She and Spartacus moved almost as one.

The dining room chairs were interspersed with stools from the kitchen, an armchair from the living room (which had been placed on the end of the table), and a swiveling desk chair from the office. The Island of Misfit Toys.

"Have a seat wherever you'd like," Caroline told George and then moved to find a seat for herself. At that moment Emily entered the room, trailed by Jane, a teenage boy who she assumed was Jake, and finally Randy.

"It's so nice of you to have us for dinner," Emily said, greeting Caroline with an embrace. "You met Jane earlier, but you didn't have a chance to meet Jake. Jake, this is Mrs. Jacobs."

"Please, call me Caroline." She reached out to shake the boy's hand. He was tall, already taller than his parents, with a bushy pile of blond hair on the top of his head. He struck Caroline as intelligent and disinterested, not unlike Polly.

"Nice to meet you," Jake said. His voice was changing. It cracked as he spoke, but he didn't seem to notice. "So you knew Mom when she was a kid. That's crazy."

"You and Emily were childhood friends?" Spartacus asked.

"We were best friends until Caroline moved," Emily said. "I was so upset when that moving truck drove away. I remember begging Caroline's mother to let her live with me."

"I'd forgotten all about that," Caroline said.

About a week after Caroline's mother had announced the move, Emily had come up with a plan. "You're not going anywhere," she had said. "Trust me."

When Penelope had arrived home from work that day, Emily, Caroline, and Lucy were sitting at the dining room table. A pot of macaroni and cheese was sitting on the stovetop, steam rising from inside. Bowls of broccoli and corn were sitting on the table.

"Look at this," her mother said as she entered the kitchen. "You guys finally decided to earn your keep."

"We just thought it would be nice if you didn't always have to make dinner," Emily said. "We know how hard you work."

"Yeah? Who told you that?"

"We can just tell," Lucy said. "You're always so cranky."

"We know how hard it is to support a family," Emily said. "We just wanted you to be able to relax a little."

"That sounds nice on paper, but I don't believe a word of it. What are you ladies up to?"

"Nothing," Caroline said. "Just trying to be nice."

"I'm serious," her mother said. "Did you burn a house down today? Get arrested for speeding?"

Lucy giggled,

"Mom, just sit."

Emily poured lemonade while Caroline scooped food onto plates. Lucy summarized *The Brady Bunch* rerun that she had been watching before dinner. They were all seated and eating when Emily made her pitch. "Mrs. Waters, we have a proposal for you."

"I knew it," she said. "Teenage girls aren't this nice without a reason. Are you a part of this?" she asked, motioning to Lucy.

She giggled again.

"Caroline and I are best friends," Emily said, launching into a formal tone. "We've lived across the street from each other forever. I know you guys aren't moving that far away, but it feels far to us. We don't want to be separated. So what I'd like to ask you for is joint custody."

"What's joint custody?" Lucy asked.

"Joint custody of Caroline?" her mother asked.

"Exactly. I'd like to have Caroline stay with me for three days a week. We can figure out which days work best, but we were thinking maybe Thursday, Friday, and Saturday, since this is when we spend the most time together anyway."

"I don't want Caroline to move away!" Lucy wailed.

"I'm not moving," Caroline said. "Just doing sleepovers."

"What do your parents think of this?" her mother asked.

"I haven't asked my parents yet," Emily said. "I figured that if you said yes, they couldn't say no."

"Very clever, but I'm afraid I'm going to have to say no for them. It's sweet, but it's just not how things work. You guys can have all the sleepovers you want, but Caroline can't live with you. Even on a part-time basis."

"But Mom," Caroline pleaded, "it's only three days a week."

"You can't get joint custody of a child just because she's moving a few miles away from her best friend. It doesn't work that way."

"We don't have to make it legal or anything," Emily said.

"Besides, I'm going to need you, Caroline. It's just the three of us now. I need you to take care of Lucy after school. We're a family. It's going to be more important than ever that we stick together."

"We didn't think about that," Emily said.

Caroline didn't care what they had and hadn't thought about. She was angry at Emily for not pushing harder. But like Emily, she knew there was no hope. That was the difference between Emily and most other children. She knew when the battle had been lost. She knew when to cut her losses. While most kids dug in their heels and fought until voices were raised, Emily understood the concept of living to fight another day.

As she listened to Emily tell the story of their joint custody proposal, Caroline suddenly found herself wondering if Emily really believed that it had been the move that ultimately doomed their friendship. How many kids attempt to negotiate for joint custody of their best friend? Maybe the person she should be angry with was her father, who was responsible for them losing the house. She'd spent so much of her life blaming a teenage girl for her problems, when in reality, it had been her father who had set things in motion. Maybe Polly was right. Maybe Emily didn't even remember the cafeteria scene. Maybe it was nothing more than a tiny blip on her radar.

"I think that's sweet," Agnes said. "Trying to get custody of your friend."

"Sweet? It was brutal," Caroline's mother said, entering the room with a pitcher of ice water in her hand. "Broke my heart. Broke my already broken heart."

"Everyone take a seat, please," Polly said, following behind her grandmother. "Mrs. Labonte, can I see you in the kitchen for a second? I could use your advice."

"Only if you call me Emily," she said.

"Of course," Polly said. Something about Polly's affability froze Caroline's heart. Something was wrong. Polly was sweet, so something had to be wrong. She rose to follow but was stopped by

Randy, who was rolling out the desk chair beside her. "No spills this time. Okay?" he said.

Caroline smiled. "Sure."

"Your daughter can really pull together a party."

"She's always been an impressive young lady," Caroline's mother said, entering the room and taking a seat beside Spartacus.

"I'm Agnes, by the way," the young woman said, waving to everyone around the table.

"I'm sorry," Caroline's mother said. "I should've introduced you. But this is better anyway. If you could just say hello when I introduce you, then Spartacus will have a sense of where everyone is sitting."

Introductions were made. It was all very friendly.

The salad bowl was making its way around the table when Polly entered the dining room. She crossed to the other side of the table a little too quickly in Caroline's estimation, and plopped down in the armchair at the far end of the table.

It was the satisfied look on her daughter's face that told Caroline that her suspicions were not unfounded. Something was amiss. Her eyes darted around the table, trying to find the trap, the snare, the spring that was about to be sprung.

It wasn't until Emily entered the dining room, holding a bottle of wine, that Caroline realized what was happening. She watched Emily stop, scan the table, and furrow her brow.

That was the moment that Caroline knew.

She could not believe Polly's ingenuity. Even as she filled with horror, she couldn't help but be impressed with her daughter.

"Where should I sit?" Emily asked, scanning the room.

Caroline knew. She didn't have to look. There were no empty seats.

A second later, Polly rose from her armchair. "Oh, dear. I dragged in every chair in the house. It looks like we don't have enough room for you, *Emily*."

Caroline began to rise, to put an end to Polly's plan, but as she did, she saw it, plain as day. A flicker of recognition on Emily's face.

She knew. And that meant she had not forgotten.

As their eyes met, it was as if the teenage version of Emily Kaplan had returned. Had never left, in fact. It had been there all along, hiding behind oatmeal cookies and admissions of possibly adulterous husbands. In that instant, the Emily Kaplan of old and the Emily Kaplan of new merged into one.

Polly had done it. Recreated history. Brought her mother back to where it had all began. It was Caroline's moment to finally say what she had wanted to say for so long.

nineteen

Caroline didn't care that this was the wrong time for a confrontation. She didn't care that her mother and her mother's boyfriend and Emily's immediate family and George Durrow and Agnes the home health aide were all listening. Emily hadn't cared about the audience around that lunch table, so Caroline didn't care now.

"This is why you brought me here?" Emily asked.

Caroline took a deep breath, preparing to fire off her own rehearsed salvo, but Emily jumped in before she could say a word. "Seriously, Caroline? You're going to embarrass me in front of my family because of a fight we had in high school?"

Caroline didn't say anything for two seconds, but in those two ticks on the clock, she felt a chasm open up, separating her from the rest of the room. The people around the table fell silent, and she could feel their collective gaze shift in her direction.

"It wasn't a fight," Caroline finally said, dropping her own gaze as she spoke. Emily's question had forced her off script. She sounded weak. Wounded. Defeated already. Polly had managed to recreate the cafeteria scene for her mother's benefit, and now it seemed that Caroline was reverting back to the same role that she had played when she was fifteen years old.

"It wasn't a fight," Caroline repeated, this time meeting Emily's gaze, hoping to find strength in her improved posture. "You humiliated me in front of my friends."

"No," Emily said. "You humiliated *yourself* in front of *my* friends. But Caroline, who cares? We were kids. It was forever ago. Don't you think you should have forgotten it by now?"

"You didn't forget," Caroline said. "You remembered. You remembered from the moment I showed up at your door. I didn't know it then, but I do now. If you never forgot about it, why would you expect me to?"

"I don't understand," Randy said. "What's going on?"

Emily sighed the sigh of the indignant and the outraged. "Caroline got stuck without a stool at lunch *back in ninth grade*, so now she's trying to get even. And apparently she's dragged her daughter into it, too."

"I'm sure we can find another seat," Spartacus said. "Right, Penny? And if not, I'm happy to give up mine."

"There's a whole dining room set in the basement," Randy said. "We could just grab a chair from there."

"How do you know there's furniture in the basement?" Emily asked.

"No," Caroline's mother said, rising from her seat. "We don't use that furniture."

"How do you know that there's a dining room set in the basement?" Emily asked again, her head now cocked in the direction of her husband.

"Caroline spilled some wine on my sweater," Randy said. We put it in the wash. The machines are in the basement."

"You didn't sit on the furniture down there?" her mother asked. "Did you?"

"No, Mom," Caroline said. "Of course not."

"When did this happen?" Emily asked.

"We can't use those chairs," Caroline's mother said again. "We don't use that furniture."

"Why not?" Jane asked, genuinely curious.

"We just don't," Caroline said.

"Don't snap at my daughter," Emily said.

"I didn't snap. We just can't use those chairs in the basement."

"Why?" Emily asked. "So you can keep me standing here like an idiot?"

"I still don't understand what's going on," Randy said.

"Your wife was a total bitch in high school," Polly said, spittle firing from her mouth. Polly was angry, and Caroline suspected that she was angrier with her than Emily. "She was mean to my mother, and it fucked up my mom's life."

"Polly!" her grandmother shouted. "Language!"

"She didn't fuck up my life," Caroline said.

"Caroline!" her mother barked.

"What's the deal then?" Emily asked. "Why am I even here?"

Polly laughed. "You can pretend that you're innocent, but I saw it on your face. And Mom did, too. I wasn't sure if she was making a big deal out of nothing, but you remembered. The second you saw that there weren't enough seats around the table, you knew. Mom was right. You were a fucking bitch in high school, and you know it."

"Hey!" Jane said, rising from her seat now. "Don't talk to my mom that way."

"Stay out of it," Polly said, not even bothering to look in Jane's direction.

"Polly!" her grandmother shouted again.

George Durrow rose from his seat, slammed both hands on the table hard enough to knock over several empty water glasses, and shouted, "Stop!" in a voice so loud, so commanding, and so unexpected that everyone froze in their tracks. All eyes (even Spartacus's, Caroline noted) turned to George, who was visibly shaking. His hands were bunched in small fists. His lips were pursed shut. The room was silent for a moment, waiting, it seemed, as George collected himself. He opened his mouth to speak, closed it, shook his head, and then opened it again. When he finally spoke, it had none of the authority of his previous command. He was quiet but earnest. Almost desperate. "I have enough bullshit in my life already," he said. "Pardon the language, Penelope, but I do. It's not every day that I get invited to a dinner party, so I'm not going to let you ruin it for me or anyone else here. So knock it off and eat some chicken."

Caroline liked George Durrow very much. She had underestimated the man.

"Fine," Emily said, the resentment in her voice receding like the ocean tide. "If I can just get a chair, I can sit down and eat." There was still hostility in her voice, but less than before. By all rights, Emily should be charging out of the room right now, but George Durrow seemed to command even her in this moment.

"Someone needs to tell me what the hell is going on," Randy said.

"I have folding chairs in the shed out back," Penelope said. "For funerals. I'll get one."

"You know what?" Polly said. "Don't bother. She can have mine." She shoved the armchair aside and stormed from the room.

"Polly!" Caroline called. "Come back here!" A second later she heard the back door slam shut.

The room was silent again. Jack, Jane, George, and Caroline's mother were still standing. Emily had yet to move from the doorway. The bottle of wine remained in her hand. After a moment, George sat back down, followed by Caroline's mother.

"George?" Emily asked. "It's George, right? I don't mean to ruin things, but I think we should leave. This is crazy. I can't stay here. My family can't stay here. But you stay. Enjoy your dinner. Maybe another time. Okay? Obviously Caroline and her daughter had other things in mind when we were invited. I think it would be better if we just left."

"Now we're leaving?" Randy said. "I don't understand what's going on."

"Me, neither," Spartacus said. "Could someone help the blind guy for Christ's sake?"

"I'll let Caroline explain," Emily said, the hostility returning to her voice. "Thank you, Mrs. Waters, for having us over. No hard feelings. Okay? Maybe Randy and I could have you over to our place sometime."

"Sure," Penelope said, uncertainly.

Emily placed the wine bottle on the table and turned to leave, pausing to allow Randy and the kids to exit ahead of her. Then she turned and faced Caroline. "I was happy to see you today. So happy. I can't imagine why you'd do something like this."

"That's how I felt in the cafeteria that day," Caroline said. "That's exactly how I felt."

"Well, I guess your plan worked then. Congratulations."

twenty

"That went well," Penelope said, pouring herself a glass of wine.

"I still have no idea what the hell happened," Spartacus said. "Could someone please explain it to me? And who's still at the table. That woman Emily and her family are gone. Right? Anyone else?"

"Polly's gone, too," Caroline's mother said. "Everyone else is present and accounted for."

"Good. Now someone please tell me what's going on."

"Caroline?" her mother said, her eyebrows raised and her head tilted to the right in a look that Caroline knew was meant to say *I told you so.* "Do you want to explain?"

Caroline felt like a fool. This whole trip had been ridiculous. She could see that now. "Can we just drop it?" she asked.

"Of course," George Durrow said.

"Absolutely not," her mother said.

"Damn straight," Spartacus said.

"Caroline was apparently still angry at Emily for something she did in high school," her mother began. "And she decided that tonight would be the night she finally said her piece. In my house. Only it didn't work out like she had planned."

"That was not my plan," Caroline said. "I had no idea what Polly was up to."

"Yes, but you're the one who dragged her to Blackstone to help you," her mother countered.

"I don't understand," George said. "Why did you need Polly's help?"

Caroline pushed back from the table. "Seriously, I don't want to talk about this."

"Too bad," her mother said. "You don't get to make the rules in this house. Answer George's question."

"I didn't need Polly's help," Caroline said. "She was in trouble at school, and I thought she could use a change of scenery. She was going to be suspended anyway, so I decided to take her with me."

"Suspended?" her mother asked.

"But Polly's the one who arranged the chairs," Agnes said.

"What do you mean *arranged the chairs*?" Spartacus asked. "How are the chairs arranged?"

"Look, I came to Blackstone to say something to Emily that I should've said a long time ago, and I was worried that I might chicken out before I got the chance. But when I went to Emily's house today, she was nothing but kind to me, and I don't know, I guess I realized that maybe I was making a mountain out of a molehill. So I decided to abandon my plan. But I told Polly that I was worried I might chicken out and to keep me on target no matter what, and that's exactly what she did."

"Like *Fargo*," Spartacus said.

"Who's Fargo?" Agnes asked.

"Not who," Spartacus said. "What. *Fargo*'s a movie. A car dealer hires a couple of thugs to kidnap his wife so he can collect the ransom from his asshole father-in-law, but at the last second, he decides to back out of the deal. He finds some money somewhere else or something. I can't remember. But he can't get in touch with the bad guys in time so they kidnap the wife anyway."

"What's that have to do with Polly?" George Durrow asked.

"Polly is just like the bad guys in the movie," Spartacus said. "You told her to do something, and now she's doing it. You can't stop her even if you wanted to."

"What happens in the movie?" Agnes asked. "To the car dealer and his wife?"

"The wife gets chopped up in a wood chipper," Spartacus said. "And the husband gets arrested, I think. I don't remember the rest."

"That's great," Caroline said. "Polly's going to end up in a wood chipper."

George Durrow raised a professorial finger. "Actually, no. Your friend Emily would be the one in the wood chipper. If we extend the analogy, I mean."

"So what would happen to Polly?" Agnes asked.

"She would be the one shoving Emily into the wood chipper," Spartacus said. "Oh, wait. Actually, it might've been Steve Buscemi in the wood chipper. At the end of the movie, one of the scumbags kills the other scumbag. So maybe Polly ends up in the wood chipper after all. Along with Emily. Though I don't think Polly is a Steve Buscemi type. She's more like the other guy. The Nordic one."

"Wait," said George. "How do you watch movies if you're blind?"

"You'd be surprised how much you can figure out just by listening. But if I'm watching with someone, we can pause the movie and they can explain what's going on. Agnes is great at that."

"That wood chipper description must have been a doozy," George said.

"Enough," Caroline said. "It's over. I had my chance here and I blew it."

"So you didn't say what you planned?" Spartacus asked.

"Not even close," Caroline said.

"Well, that's good," Spartacus said, grinning.

"Why?"

"Because what you said sucked," he said. "I mean, you ambushed the poor girl and she still got the best of you as far as I could tell."

"Thanks a lot," Caroline said.

George Durrow cleared his throat. "Caroline, I know it didn't work out like you envisioned, but I think it was pretty brave of you to give it a try. I think a lot of us would like a second chance with a high school bully. You at least gave yourself a chance."

Caroline shook her head. "I guess things don't change much."

"You're just figuring that out now, sweetie?" Spartacus said with a laugh.

Caroline glared at him before she realized that Spartacus was immune to all forms of passive-aggressive facial expressions. No wonder he got along with her mother so well.

"Emily was right," her mother said. "You've got to let it go. Kids do stupid things. You can't blame her for the rest of her life. She's a different person now."

"I don't buy that," Caroline snapped. "You are who you are."

"That's a tough way to live your life, sweetie, never forgiving anyone for the indiscretions of their youth," Spartacus said.

Or forgiving yourself.

Only now did Caroline understand why she had returned to Blackstone. Emily had been the impetus, but she wasn't the real reason for this journey. Spartacus was right. It's a tough way to live, never forgiving anyone for the indiscretions of their youth. Especially yourself.

Her journey home was about a secret. Her secret. The burden that she had been carrying on her back for so long. The guilt she had carried for so long.

The secret behind Lucy's death was more important than anything Emily had done to her. She had blamed Emily for her sister's death, and though she still believed that Emily owned a small part of it, that part was shrinking fast. The reason she had hid that plastic bag in Lucy's closet and never spoke the truth about that day was because Caroline was responsible for her sister's death, more than Emily and even more than Katherine Paley, who she had last seen standing beside that yellow van in the middle of Summer

Street on the day her sister died, but who she suddenly wanted
to see again.

In that moment, she knew why she had brought Polly here in
the first place. She needed someone to tell. It was time to dig that
plastic bag out from her sister's closet, open it, and tell someone
what she had done.

twenty-one

When Caroline heard Tom's voice from somewhere in the house, she rolled over and wrapped her arms around her pillow. Pulled the other pillow over her head to muffle the sound. Why did he have to be so loud in the morning? Couldn't the man sleep in for once in her life?

Then it hit her.

"Tom?"

She looked across the room to Polly's empty bed.

Caroline dressed quickly and made her way downstairs. She found Tom in the kitchen engaged in conversation with her mother.

"What are you doing here?"

"It's nice to see you, too," he said, stepping across the room to hug her. Tom looked tired. Tired eyes. Uncombed hair. Wrinkled shirt.

"Seriously," she said. "What are you doing here?"

"You didn't answer your phone all day yesterday, so I canceled my appointments for the next couple days and drove up."

"You drove all night?"

"Actually, I went to bed early, got up at two in the morning, and pulled into your mother's driveway just before nine. No traffic if you travel at the right time."

"It's nine?" Caroline asked, looking to the clock on the wall for clarification.

"Nine forty-five," her mother said. She was standing at the stove, laying strips of bacon into a sizzling pan.

"Where's Polly?"

"I assumed she was still sleeping with you," her mother said. "She's not?"

"No, and the bed's still made."

"Maybe she made it before she left," her mother said.

"Polly's never made a bed in her life," Tom and Caroline said in unison.

"If she didn't sleep in the bed last night, where did she sleep?" Tom asked.

"I don't know," Caroline said.

"I'll check the bed," her mother said. "I'll be able to tell if she made it or not. Watch the bacon, Tom. I don't want a grease fire."

Caroline waited until her mother had left the kitchen before speaking. "I can't believe you drove all this way. You didn't need to come."

"I thought you might need me."

She had expected Tom to chastise her for her sudden and unprecedented disappearance. Now she felt bad for doubting him. "I'm fine. Really."

"Can you tell me what's going on?"

"It's going to sound stupid," Caroline said. "But at the time, it made a lot of sense."

"Okay."

She explained the events of the previous day as she poured coffee and sat down across from Tom at the small kitchen table.

"I can't believe I never told you about it," Caroline said. It didn't feel like much of a secret anymore. She felt foolish for not telling anyone sooner. "It was something Emily did in high school. A long story. I hadn't spoken to her in years, but then something came up, and I felt like now was the right time to confront her. I know. It sounds so stupid when I say it out loud."

"Mary Kate Dinali," Tom asked. "She's the something that came up?"

The problem solver at work.

Caroline leaned across the table and kissed him. "Yes, Mary Kate was part of it. But there's more."

"Do you want to talk about it?"

"She didn't sleep in that bed last night," Penelope said, reentering the kitchen. "There's no way in hell that Polly made those hospital corners."

"I don't understand," Tom said. "Did she stay with a friend?"

"She doesn't know anyone in town," Penelope said.

"Where could she be then?" Tom asked.

"I'll call her," Caroline said, pulling her phone from her pocket. "Did you check Lucy's room?"

"Yes, and the attic, too," her mother said. "Did you see her at all after she stormed out last night?"

"Stormed out?" Tom said.

"No," Caroline said, avoiding Tom's question. "Did you?"

"No," her mother said. "I went to bed around ten."

"She's not answering," Caroline said.

"I don't understand," Tom said again. "If she doesn't know anyone in town, where could she be?"

"I said I don't know."

"You said she stormed out of the house," Tom said. "When did that happen?"

"At dinner. Around six."

"So Polly's been gone since six last night?"

Panic formed in the pit of Caroline's stomach. "God, where could she be?"

"There's no one she could've stayed with?" Tom asked. "No one at all?"

"She knows George and Spartacus," Penelope said. "She doesn't know where they live, but she called them yesterday to invite them to dinner, so she might still have their phone numbers. Let me phone them. I have George's number in my office." She headed down the hallway toward her office.

"Who are George and Spartacus?" Tom asked.

"I'll tell you later," Caroline said. "You should try calling Polly. She was pissed at me when she left yesterday. Maybe she'll pick up for you."

Tom pulled his phone from his pocket. "Why was she mad at you?"

"I let her down. It's part of my long story. Is it ringing?"

"Yes. She's not picking up."

"George and Spartacus haven't seen her since she left last night," her mother said as she returned to the room, and for the first time, Caroline could hear fear in her mother's voice, too. It frightened her. She turned to Tom. "What should we do?"

"I'll call Dino," her mother said. "He'll know what to do."

Officer Dean "Dino" Dugan was a thick, hairy man who chewed gum like he wanted to make it suffer. He was wearing his uniform when he stepped through the front door. The sudden appearance of his badge and gun somehow made Polly's disappearance feel real—and much more serious.

"So there's no custody issues of any kind?" Dugan asked.

"No," Tom said.

"And the last time you saw your daughter was when she left the house in the middle of dinner?"

"Yes," Caroline said.

"And she doesn't have a boyfriend or any friends that you know of in Blackstone? Or anywhere around here. Correct?"

"We've only been here for two days," Caroline said. "She doesn't even have a boyfriend back in Maryland."

"Not one that you know of," Dugan said. "Wasn't she here last summer?"

"Yes," Penelope said. "She was. She stayed with me for about a month. That's right. You met Polly. Didn't you?"

Dugan nodded. "Yup. Nice girl. I knew I was going to have to put Buster down, so I came here first to make arrangements. Your daughter was a real sweetheart."

This made Caroline like the man a little bit more. It made him feel less like a badge and a gun and more like a human being.

"More important," Dugan continued, "it means she could've met someone when she was here last summer. A boy, even. I assume you didn't have her under surveillance twenty-four hours a day, Penny?"

"No. In fact, she had the place to herself for the weekend when I went to the Mohegan Sun with my friend Lisa."

"So it's possible that she stayed with a friend, either because that's what she planned to do all along or because she was so pissed off at you that she didn't want to come home."

Caroline had underestimated Officer Dugan.

"So what should we do now?" Tom asked.

"Hold on," Dugan said. "We're not done. Has she been out of your sight since you arrived yesterday?"

Caroline thought for a moment. "She walked back here yesterday after we visited Emily."

"Why?" Tom asked.

"She was pissed at me. Refused to get back in the car. I know. It sounds like all we've done is fight, but things were actually going well."

Dugan shook his head. "If we wanted to, we could probably label every teenager in the world bipolar and lock them up in the psych ward until they're old enough to vote," Dugan said. "Might be better for everyone involved. One minute they love you. The next minute they never want to speak to you again."

Caroline smiled.

"I have two myself. A girl and a boy. Most days they drive me crazy, but I'd run through fire for them if I had to."

Caroline liked this man.

"So where does this Emily live?" Dugan asked.

"Over by the high school. Emily Kaplan. I mean, Emily Labonte."

"Oh," Dugan said, smiling. "Emily and Randy. You visited them yesterday?"

"Yes. And Emily's daughter, Jane, took Polly to that place across the street from the high school."

"The Spot," Dugan said. "So it's possible that Polly met someone there, too. That place is lousy with kids after school."

"I guess so," Caroline said. "I hadn't even thought of that. But it's not like Polly to make friends easily."

"You have a picture of Polly?" Dugan asked.

"Yeah," Tom said. "Lots of them. On my phone."

"Good. E-mail a couple of them to me." Dugan handed Tom a business card. "Send it to that address, and I'll forward it to the department. There's only six of us, but Blackstone isn't that big a place, and we know most everyone. We'll get the word out. Honestly, though. She's probably fine. Just a pissed-off kid trying to make you crazy."

"What should we do?" Tom asked.

"Keep calling her. If she hasn't come back by six, we'll meet again. And one of you should go over to the Labontes' house and see if their daughter knows anything. She'll be in school right now, and I'd rather not have a cop show up and pull her out of class to ask a few questions. She's more likely to be candid without me there. At least at first. Besides, I can't legally talk to her without her parents' permission. But Emily can go over to the school and get her out of class for a few minutes without starting any rumors. What's her name again?"

"Jane," Caroline said.

"If they were at The Spot together and Polly met someone, Jane will know it. And she might've told Polly about some of her hangouts, too. Places where she and her friends go. Polly could be holed up in one of those places, too. When I was a kid, my friends and I hung out at Harris Pond or High Rocks, but there must be a hundred places in town where kids hang out. See if Jane mentioned any of them to Polly. If you feel like Jane is holding back on you, I can question her after school if Emily gives me consent."

"Anything else?" Tom asked.

"Try not to worry," Dugan said. "Ninety-nine percent of the time, a kid disappears for a day or two to blow off steam. But eventually they get hungry or cold and come home with their tail between their legs. Your daughter's a smart cookie. Treated me real nice when I was going through a rough patch. I'm sure she's just being her stupid teenage self right now. They can't help it."

"What about the other one percent?" Tom asked.

"We don't have those in Blackstone," Dugan said.

Officer Dugan shook Tom and Caroline's hands, gave Penelope a bear hug, and left, promising to call back as soon as he heard anything.

As soon as the door closed, Tom said, "I'm going to try Polly from the house phone. Maybe she'll pick up if she thinks it's her grandmother."

"I doubt it," Penelope said. Then she turned to Caroline. "Looks like you're going to have to make nice with your old friend after all."

twenty-two

Emily was dressed impeccably in a cashmere sweater, silk scarf, jeans, and leopard-print ballet flats. Even her hair was done up in a perfect French twist. Had Caroline ever answered the door looking this good?

Emily's smile evaporated upon seeing Caroline. "Seriously?" she said, taking two steps back into the house. "Aren't we finished already?"

"I'm sorry to bother you—"

"Sorry to bother me?" Emily interjected. "You had no problem ambushing me in front of a bunch of strangers last night. You call this a bother?"

"I didn't know it was happening last night," Caroline said. "Polly planned the whole thing. I was just as surprised as you."

"You're blaming your daughter now?"

"She's missing," Caroline said, hoping to detour the argument. "Polly never came home last night."

Emily blinked. "Oh, I'm sorry to hear that." Then just as quickly, she seemed to steel herself once again. "But she's not here."

"No, I didn't think she would be. But the police suggested that I speak to Jane. She might know something."

"Why would Jane know anything?"

"Polly could've met someone at The Spot yesterday. Or maybe Jane mentioned some place in Blackstone that the kids like to go. Polly doesn't know Blackstone all that well, so unless she slept on the street last night, she had to hook up with someone at some point or be given an idea about a good place to hang out. I'm hoping Jane knows something."

"Jane isn't home," Emily said.

"I know. The police suggested . . . well, I was wondering if you would pull her from class for a few minutes so I could talk to her. They—the police, that is—said it would be better than sending a cop over to the school to question her."

"Not to mention that would be illegal," Emily said, any empathy now completely gone from her voice.

"I don't know what's legal and what's not," Caroline said. "I just want to find Polly."

Emily folded her arms over her chest.

Caroline took a step forward. "Look, I know what happened last night wasn't good. I'm sorry. I honestly didn't know it was happening until all hell broke loose."

"But isn't that why you came to Blackstone? To confront me?"

"Yes," Caroline admitted. "But once I actually saw you . . . after we talked . . . well, I decided to forget the whole thing. It was a stupid idea. But I made the mistake of telling Polly about it, and she refused to let it go."

"It was a lousy thing to do, you know."

So was that cafeteria bullshit, Caroline thought but knew better than to say at this moment. "I know it was. But Polly's missing and I need your help. Please."

"Fine," Emily said stepping back from the door. "Come in."

"But if you don't mind," she said, "we really can't wait for Jane to come home. The police said we should pull her from class."

"I understand," Emily said. "Just hold on a minute." She disappeared in the direction of the kitchen, leaving Caroline in the foyer.

Caroline waited a moment before deciding to follow.

"I know this is awkward," she called as she entered the kitchen. Emily was standing by an open drawer at the far counter, shuffling papers. "I wouldn't be here if it wasn't important."

Emily put the papers on the countertop and turned. "That's a shame, then. Had you handled things differently, we might be friends again."

"Had *I* handled things differently? I wasn't the one who stopped being your friend."

"Jesus Christ, Caroline!" Emily said. "Can't you let it go? We were kids. It was one fight. One stupid fight a million years ago. And you were being just as bitchy as I was that day."

"One fight?" Caroline said. "You never spoke to me again. You barely even looked at me again after that day. Even after what happened to Lucy, you never said a word to me."

Old bullets. It felt good to fire them. "This is ridiculous," Emily said. "All I wanted to do is to let the new girl sit with us for one day, and you acted like I started World War III."

"That was not just any new girl," Caroline said. "That was Ellie fucking Randolph."

"What's that supposed to mean?"

"I didn't see you inviting Amy Silver to the lunch table," Caroline said. "You never gave her the time of day."

"Amy Silver?"

"Yeah, the girl from Wisconsin with no chest and bangs."

"Oh, God," Emily said, managing a smile. "I'd forgotten about her."

"Forgot about her? You never even knew her. I only remember Amy because when you stopped being my friend, I stopped going to lunch, and I'd see her in the library sometimes. Skipping lunch like me."

"I didn't make you skip lunch."

"I had six friends in the world, Emily. *Six*. And you were my best friend. You abandoned me and took every single one of them with you."

Emily sighed. "I just wanted a little space. I didn't think that one lunch period was going to end everything."

"That's bullshit and you know it," Caroline said, pointing her finger across the granite countertop at Emily. "That wasn't one lunch. You dumped me. And you took Molly and Briana and the rest of them with you. Right when I needed you the most."

"Enough," Emily said, turning back to the papers on the countertop. "I don't want to argue about ancient history. Okay? Let's just go talk to Jane and get this over with."

"No, it's not *enough*. It sucked, Emily. High school was hell for me because of that day."

"Jesus Christ, Caroline. You could've made some new friends. You act like it was me or nothing."

Caroline didn't speak. She was afraid that if she did, she might crack.

Emily turned. "What?"

Caroline steeled herself, tightening her lips and lowering her voice. "It *was* you or nothing."

"Caroline, we were friends because we lived next door to each other when we were little kids. But it's not like we had much in common. You didn't care about the same things I cared about. We were just different people, and we drifted apart. It happens. It's not a crime."

Caroline opened her mouth, ready to end this. *You're right,* she would say. Just agree so they could go find Polly. But it was the thought of Polly that changed her mind. "No," she said, anger returning to her voice. "I'm sorry, but what happened in that cafeteria isn't called *drifting apart*. That was something else."

"Do you think I'm happy about what happened that day?" Emily said.

"Do you even remember what happened that day?"

"Of course I do! Jesus Christ, Caroline. You were my best friend since I was five. What kind of fucking monster do you think I am?"

"When you saw me yesterday, you acted like nothing had happened. Nothing at all."

"I was happy to see you. What'd you expect?"

"Let's just get going. Okay?" Caroline said. She didn't want to argue anymore. "Polly's been gone since dinner last night and I'm worried."

"Fine. I came in here to check Jane's schedule. See what class she's in now."

"You have her class schedule?" Caroline wasn't even sure about what classes Polly was taking.

"Of course I do," she said, shuffling through the papers in front of her. "Hold on." A second later, she shook her head and laughed.

"What?"

"Guess where she is right now?"

twenty-three

So much had happened. And so little had changed.

It had been more than two decades since Caroline had attended Blackstone-Millville Regional High School. Okay, everything seemed a little smaller and a little dingier than she remembered, but other than that, everything was the same. Same color schemes. Same fluorescent lighting. Same industrial smell. The brick appeared a little less red. The sidewalk appeared a little more cracked, but so much just seemed frozen in time. Even the trees in the courtyard: short, thin, frail-looking things, were exactly the same as she remembered.

"They must be so depressed by all the gray concrete that they don't grow," Caroline said.

"What?" Emily asked.

"Never mind."

Four women sat behind the counter inside the school's office. Each stood and greeted Emily by name. Each inquired about Jane, Jack, and Randy.

"We need to chat with Jane for a couple minutes, if that's okay," Emily said, directing her comment to the woman closest to the counter.

"Sure. Let me just see where she is," the woman said.

"No need," Emily said, waving the woman off. "She's at lunch. I checked before we drove over."

"Oh, okay then. You know where that is."

"Yes, we do," Emily said. "Oh, I'm sorry. This is Caroline Jacobs. She's a BMR alum, too."

"Is Jacobs your maiden name?" one of the older women near the back of the office asked.

"No. I was Caroline Waters when I went here."

At the mention of Caroline's maiden name, the woman's face changed. Her eyes widened ever so slightly. Her head tilted to the side. Her lips grew thin. Caroline knew this look well. It was the *You're the sister of the dead girl* look. "Caroline Waters," the woman said. "I remember you."

"That was a long time ago. You have a good memory."

The woman smiled. "You sit here long enough, you get a brain for names and faces."

"I'm sure," Caroline said.

After signing in and placing a visitor sticker on her shirt (Emily stuck hers on the thigh of her jeans, which felt like the cool thing to do), they made their way to the cafeteria on the other side of the school.

They took the stairs to the first floor and crossed through the lobby where the school's glass trophy case was positioned between the doors to the auditorium. Caroline stopped to look. Trophies and plaques with names of people she once knew were still standing among dozens of others, somehow collecting dust in the sealed glass case. The marching band's NESBA championship in 1986. The plaque commemorating the cross-country team's national record for most consecutive victories. A photo of the school's only Division C championship basketball team, led by team captain and point guard Randy Labonte.

He looked so young back then. They all did.

The sounds of the cafeteria hadn't changed in a quarter century, either. A hum of excitement filled the room, punctuated by the occasional laugh, shout, or clattering of a lunch tray striking the floor. Even the smells were the same. The strangely sweet combination of floor wax, spoiled milk, and too many teenaged bodies in too small a space brought Caroline right back to her high school days.

The tables and attached stools appeared unchanged as well. They were the same ones that she had sat on as a kid, or at least an identical set. Those goddamn orange disks.

A woman stepped over to where Caroline and Emily were standing in the doorway. "Can I help you?" She was a teacher, Caroline knew, but also young. Fresh out of college. She couldn't remember a teacher ever looking this young when she was in high school.

"Yes," Emily said. "I'm here to speak to my daughter for a second. Nancy in the office said I could come down."

"Oh. Okay, do you know where she sits during lunch?"

"No," Emily said. "Want me to just look around?"

"Who's your daughter?"

"Jane Labonte," Emily said.

"Oh, Jane!" the woman said. "I know where she sits. I'm Ms. Bennett, Jane's English teacher from last year." She reached out and shook Emily's hand. "Such a wonderful daughter you have."

Emily smiled. "Ms. Bennett. Sorry, I should've recognized you. Jane adored your class. Could you show me where she's sitting? We're in kind of a rush. Something important."

"Of course. Jane's in the middle. Over there."

Caroline followed the woman's hand and spotted Jane, about twenty feet from where she and Emily had once sat together.

"I'll just send her over here, if you'd like."

"That'd be great," Emily said.

Ms. Bennett turned and headed in the direction of Jane and her friends.

"It's kind of unbelievable that we're standing here in the cafeteria again. Considering the circumstances."

"Tell me about it," Caroline said and smiled. "If Ellie was here, this could be an episode of *The Twilight Zone*."

Jane looked up, saw her mother at the doorway, and smiled.

Waved. Stood up and walked over with an actual skip in her step. Caroline had to give Emily credit. Had she showed up at Polly's school during lunch, a smile and a wave would be the last things she would expect from her daughter.

"Mom," Jane said. "Is everything okay?" She was avoiding eye contact with Caroline.

"Everything's fine, honey."

"Everything's fine?" Caroline asked.

"Sorry," Emily said, turning to Caroline. "You know what I mean." Then she turned back to Jane. "Listen, Polly is missing. She didn't go home last night after the dinner, and we're just wondering if you might know where she went?"

"Me? Why would I know where she went?"

"Not that you'd know," Caroline said. "But Polly doesn't know Blackstone well, so we were wondering if you might've mentioned a place where she could've gone last night. A place where kids hang out nowadays?"

"No," Jane said. "Nothing like that."

"Did she meet anyone when you took her to The Spot?" Caroline asked. "Someone she could've called last night when she needed a place to stay?"

"No. I saw a couple of my friends there, and I introduced her to them, but it's not like they exchanged phone numbers or anything. Besides, I was in class with Jenny and Samantha last period. I think they would've said something if Polly showed up at their door last night."

"Can you just think for a minute," Caroline said. "Was there anything you said that might've given her an idea about where to go last night? Anything at all?"

Jane was silent for a moment. Caroline gave the girl credit. She had the right to act like a bitch but seemed to be genuinely trying to help. "Nothing that I can think of," Jane said, shaking her head. "Honestly. We just talked about school and stuff."

"Okay," Emily said. "Thanks for trying."

"Sure," Jane said. "I'd better get back. Lunch is over in a couple minutes." She turned to head back to her table and then turned back, directing her attention at Caroline. "I think it was awful what you did to my mom last night, but I hope you find her. And I'm sure she's okay."

"Why's that?" Caroline said.

"Polly's tough," Jane said. "She could probably live in the woods for a month, eating squirrels and drinking from puddles, and it wouldn't faze her. She probably didn't come home last night just to spite you."

Caroline smiled. "You sound like you have some experience with this kind of thing."

"No, I wouldn't have the guts to do something like that. But Polly does."

Ten minutes later they were climbing back into Caroline's car. "So now what?" Emily said.

Caroline sighed. "I hope Jane's right. It's funny. I should probably be more worried than I am, but I guess I sort of agree with her. For all her faults, Polly's tough as nails."

"Is this something Polly would do?" Emily asked. "Stay out all night just to worry you?"

"She's never done it before, but yeah. I could see that."

"So?"

Caroline shrugged. "I guess I go back to my mother's house and wait."

"Do you want me to go with you? Keep you company?"

"You don't have to do that. Tom's here. He showed up last night."

"Your husband?" Emily asked.

"Yeah. He got worried. I wasn't returning calls. And I sort of disappeared without warning."

"Like mother, like daughter."

Caroline smiled. "Yeah, I guess so. But thanks for the offer."

"Sure. It's strange. Huh?"

"What?"

"All this," Emily said. "I feel like I want to hug you and kill you in the same second."

"Yeah. Exactly."

An open palm struck the Caroline's passenger side window, causing her to jump. She turned. It was Jane, staring wide-eyed.

"Sorry," she shouted through the glass.

Caroline lowered the window.

"Sorry," she repeated. "I didn't mean to scare you. It's just that I thought of something."

"What?" Caroline asked.

"We did talk about a place. Not exactly a hangout, but it might be worth a try."

twenty-four

"I can't believe it's still here," Caroline said, staring up into the tree.

"It's built with pressure-treated lumber," Emily said. "What did you expect?"

"How do you know what pressure-treated lumber is?" Caroline asked.

Emily opened her mouth to answer but Caroline cut her short.

"Never mind. You'll just make me feel stupid. Stupider than I already feel."

Emily smiled. "We built that deck onto the house a few years ago. I learned about it then. Your father built this. Right?"

"Yup. The only decent thing the man ever did that I'm aware of."

"Do you know where he is today?"

"Dead," Caroline said. "Heart attack."

"I'm sorry."

"It's okay," Caroline said. "I only found out that he died because of his will."

"Didn't make you rich, huh?"

"He left me four hundred dollars. I gave it to charity."

The two stood silent for a moment. Caroline stared at the tree house, wondering how a man who could put so much of his time and effort into something like this could just disappear two years later. He loved her enough to build something to last a quarter century but couldn't stick around long enough to keep it in the family. Tears welled in her eyes. She knew that she wasn't the best · parent in the world, and there were days when she felt like she was the worst, but she never felt as bad as her own father had been.

"Do you think Polly's up there?"

Caroline shrugged She cupped her hands over her mouth and shouted in the direction of the tree house. "Polly!"

"Could she be ignoring you?" Emily asked.

"That's entirely possible."

"Should we go up and check?"

"You mean climb the tree?" Caroline asked.

"Yeah. It looks safe." Emily motioned to the rectangular wedges that had been nailed into the tree to form a ladder.

"Let me guess," Caroline said. "Pressure-treated wood?"

"Probably. But I bet that ladder has been replaced since our day. The nail heads don't look rusted and the wood looks too new. I'm sure it's safe. C'mon. Let's go up."

"I don't know if I can."

"Oh, c'mon," Emily said. "Don't make me start bullying you again."

Caroline couldn't help herself. She smiled. It took a couple minutes for the two of them to negotiate the ladder and emerge through a hole in the platform and onto the deck.

"It looks so small," Emily said, ducking her head to avoid a tree limb. "Not like I remember."

"I know. I can't believe our parents used to let us play up here. It's so dangerous. We could've fallen off easy."

Emily laughed. "My mom used to drive us around in the back of her pickup truck. Remember? This was nothing."

Caroline stepped over to the tree house and peered inside the doorway. "Polly?"

"No luck?" Emily asked.

"Wait." Caroline crouched even lower and went inside. At the other side of the room was a small plastic bag from CVS and a large, yellow envelope.

"What is it?" Emily asked, poking her head through the door.

"Polly was here," Caroline said, holding up the bag and the envelope.

"How do you know?"

Caroline opened the bag so Emily could see the inside. "Charleston Chews and Red Bull. That's Polly." She raised the envelope. "And this is mine. She must've lifted it from my purse."

"I didn't even know they still made Charleston Chews. I used to love them."

"I remember," Caroline said. "We both did."

"There's one left," Emily said. "Want to split it?"

"Sure."

"What's in the envelope?" Emily asked.

"Photographs. Some of my work."

"Can I see?"

She passed the envelope across to Emily and sat down, feeling unexpected butterflies in her stomach.

Emily pulled out half a dozen large glossy prints and flipped through them, pausing for a moment on each one. "These are amazing," Emily said. "The way you catch the light on the web is so beautiful. I had no idea that you were so talented."

"Thanks," Caroline said. A compliment from Emily meant so much. Caroline hated herself for it.

Late morning was transitioning to early afternoon. The sun had moved almost directly overhead, casting them in dark shadows. Emily pulled the candy bar apart and handed a piece to Caroline. "So that's good," she said. "Polly probably spent the night here just to spite you, like Jane said. She might be on her way to your mom's house right now."

"Yeah. I should text Tom and let him know." She removed her phone from her pocket and began typing.

"This must be weird for you," Emily said. "This was your tree house first, and now it belongs to some other kid."

"Do you know that a kid even lives here?"

"Guess not," Emily said. "Polly might've been the first person to use it in a long time."

Caroline smiled. She and Emily had assumed the same positions they did as children, sitting opposite one another, a candy bar between them. "Those were such good days," she said.

"They were," Emily said between bites.

"Until I married Tom and had Polly, those were probably my best days," Caroline said.

Caroline saw the tears but couldn't believe it. But they were there, pouring down Emily's cheeks like two tiny rivers.

"I didn't mean to drag you up here and make you cry. It's fine. Seriously, Emily. I didn't mean—"

"Don't." She held up her hand, motioning Caroline to stop. To wait. She took a deep breath and wiped the tears from her eyes. "Do you remember the day I broke my leg and you dragged me home?"

"You broke your ankle. Not your leg. And I didn't drag you home. I dragged you to the Benders' house. Our parents were at work."

"You're right," Emily said. "I forgot about that. Actually I'd forgotten about that whole day until you mentioned how dangerous it was up here for kids."

"Okay?" Caroline wasn't sure where this was going.

Emily wiped away more tears. "You're right," she said, her soft voice quavering. "I was awful."

Caroline didn't know what to say.

"I've known it forever," Emily said. "And I know you're going to want to punch me in the face for saying this, but it's been hard on me, too."

"You're right," Caroline said. "I do want to punch you. Apparently it runs in my family."

"I know it's awful to say, but it's true. I avoid this street whenever I can so I don't have to drive by your old house. And I've never brought my kids to Harris Pond because I can't stand all the memories of the two of us there. And I try to avoid the cafeteria at the high school whenever I can. They have all these fruit punch and cookie receptions after concerts and soccer games, but I'm always trying to skip them. I can't stand to even think about that place."

"Then why do you keep telling me to get over it?"

"Because when your oldest friend shows up on your doorstep claiming that you ruined her life, it's not exactly the easiest thing to accept, even if you regret what you did. I always knew that I had acted like a bitch, but I had no idea how badly I had ruined things for you."

"You didn't ruin things."

"I didn't make it any easier," Emily said. "You said so your-self."

Part of her wanted to tell Emily that it was meaningless high school drama that happens all the time, but she stopped. She wasn't going to pretend for the sake of Emily. "No," she said again. "It didn't make it any easier."

"I know. I still can't believe what I did."

"Why, Em? Why did you do it?"

Emily took a moment to collect herself. When she began speaking this time, it was almost in a whisper. "You were shy. And kind of awkward." She paused for a moment, and then even softer, almost inaudible, "And poor." She shook her head. "You get one chance at high school. Four years and that's it. And I wanted it to be good. I wanted to be popular. I wanted it to be like it is in the movies. And you know what? It was. I had to be a bitch to make it happen, but I married my high school sweetheart and the captain of the baseball team. I was prom queen during our junior and se-nior year. As awful as I was, Jane and Jack wouldn't exist today if I hadn't done the things I did."

"You think that you and Randy wouldn't be together today if you hadn't dumped me that day in the cafeteria."

"Yeah," Emily said. "I do. I didn't just dump you that day. That was the day I decided that I was going to be popular no matter what it took. I had one chance at making high school great and I was going to take it."

"Even if it meant hurting me in the process," Caroline said.

"Yeah, I guess so. And look where it's got me. My prom king is going to leave me for some younger woman."

"You don't know that," Caroline said.

"I kind of do."

They sat in silence for a while, gnawing on Charleston Chews and staring at the floorboards. Caroline found herself mesmerized by the simplicity of Emily's rationale. She wanted to be popular, and that meant ditching her shy, awkward, poor friend in the pursuit of popularity. It made sense. As cruel as it was, it made perfect sense.

It happened in the movies all the time.

She wondered if she would've done the same thing had she been in Emily's place. No. Not a chance in hell. She was a lot of things (or maybe not enough things), but she was not a bully. Even in the pursuit of popularity, she never would have done what Emily did.

And how much blame should Emily assume for Lucy's death? Half? More than half?

None, Caroline thought with certainty. Not one bit. I own it all.

In that moment she knew, with equal certainty, that if she ever told Emily the truth about Lucy's death, Emily might try to assume some of the blame. Perhaps all of it. She could never allow that to happen. She would tell Polly, because that still felt right. But she would protect Emily from the truth, even if a small, angry part of her wanted Emily to know everything.

"Caroline?" Emily said, her voice soft again.

"Yeah?"

"I'm sorry. I'm sorry for what I did that day and for all the days after that day. I wish I could make it up to you. Give you all those years back."

Caroline smiled. She didn't know it until just now, but she had been waiting for Emily to apologize. Not only for the past two days but for the past twenty-five years. And in this tree house, on this day, in this moment, it finally happened. She stood and reached her arms out to embrace her friend, and as she did, her head slammed into a crossbeam in the ceiling, sending her sprawling back down to the floor. "Ouch!" she shouted, grabbing the top of her head, which was already throbbing in pain. And then she burst into laughter. Bubbling, teary-eyed, uncontrollable laughter. A second later Emily was laughing, too. Then Emily crawled across the tree house to Caroline and wrapped her arms around her friend. The two of them lay on the floor of their childhood hangout, laughing and crying.

twenty-five

"What's going on up there? Is everyone okay?"

Caroline recognized the voice.

"She's bleeding," the woman standing beside Officer Dugan said. She was a short, middle-aged woman wearing a pink robe and slippers. And she was shaking an empty coffee cup up at the tree house. The woman's blond hair was in what Caroline thought were rollers, though she had never actually seen rollers in real life. She looked like something out of a 1950s sitcom. "Who's bleeding?" Caroline asked.

"You're bleeding," the woman shouted. "You're bleeding all over my tree house." Then she turned to Officer Dugan. "That woman is bleeding all over my tree house."

Caroline didn't like the way the woman had said *my tree house*.

"It's true," Emily said, looking up. "Your forehead is bleeding like hell."

"What in the name of God were you two doing up there?" the woman asked.

Caroline touched her forehead. It was wet and sticky. She looked at her hand. Her fingertips were spotted with blood. "I must have cut it when I hit my head on that beam."

"Can you climb down?" Officer Dugan asked.

"Of course."

"Do you feel light-headed?" he asked.

"No. I'm fine. I'm coming down."

"Wait," he said, holding his hand out like a traffic cop. "Maybe I should get the fire department out here. Just to be safe."

"Don't you dare," Caroline said, moving to the ladder and beginning her descent.

"I'm not going to let you drive a fire engine over my lawn," the woman snapped at Dugan.

"Relax, Barbara," Officer Dugan said.

"Don't tell me to relax."

"We were just looking for my friend's daughter," Emily said. "We thought she might've been hiding in the tree house. My friend used to live here when she was a kid."

"That doesn't just give you permission to traipse around my backyard."

"We knocked on your door," Caroline said, finally joining Emily, Dugan, and Barbara. "You didn't answer."

"I was sleeping. I'm home sick today. But just because I didn't answer the door doesn't mean you can trespass on my property."

"Barbara has a problem with kids using her tree house," Dugan explained. "It happens a lot."

"Smoking. Drinking. God knows what happens up there."

"You're really bleeding," Emily said, leaning in close to examine Caroline's scalp. She turned to Barbara. "Do you have a first-aid kit?"

"I have one in the cruiser," Dugan said. "I'll go get it."

"I'm coming with you," Barbara said. The two crossed the backyard and turned the corner at the edge of the house. A second later, Emily and Caroline were alone.

"I'm worried about Polly," Caroline said.

"Don't be," Emily said. "We know she was here last night. She's probably on her way back to your mother's place right now."

"I can't stand the thought of her sleeping in that tree house alone."

Emily laughed. "I did it on more than one occasion. It's uncomfortable but not all that bad."

"You did? When?"

"When I was in high school," Emily said. "I got along with my parents for the most part, but things weren't always rosy. When I would run away from home, I would come here and spend the night. I didn't know it at the time, but my parents always knew where I was."

"I had no idea that you used to run away from home."

"Not really running away," Emily said. "More like a cooling down period. You know teenagers. Everything has to be dramatic. You never came back here after you moved?"

"I couldn't even stand the thought of seeing this place. I missed it so much. Still do. This was the last place that I can remember being perfectly happy."

"You're not happy now?"

"I'm happy," Caroline said. "It's been a tough few years for me and Polly. We fight a lot. Actually, we used to fight a lot. Now we just don't talk. But that's normal, I guess. So yeah, I'm happy. But I'm talking about that special brand of perfect childhood happiness. You know what I mean? When the only thing you worried about was getting home before the street lights came on."

"I don't know if I ever had a time when I felt like that. My childhood was great, but there was always a lot of pressure to get good grades. And my parents fought a lot. I think they put all of their attention and effort on me so they wouldn't have to focus on each other."

"Are they still together?" Caroline asked, surprised and a little embarrassed that it had taken her this long to ask. For a good portion of her childhood, they had been like surrogate parents to her.

"No, they got divorced after I graduated. I think they were waiting until I moved out to split. Dad lives in Maine. He got remarried to a woman he met online. A sheep farmer, if you can believe it. I actually like her a lot. He moved onto her farm. He shears sheep and raises chickens now."

"I can't imagine your father raising chickens," Caroline said. "That's wild."

"Right," Emily said. "No blue suits needed on a farm."

"And your mom?" Caroline asked. "What about her?"

"She lives on the Cape. Bought a bed-and-breakfast and works her ass off every summer so she can spend the winter on the couch, reading and knitting."

"Is she married?" Caroline asked.

"No. She's had a few boyfriends, but nothing's stuck."

"I always thought your parents had the perfect marriage."

Emily laughed. "They did a good job of faking it for the benefit of the world, but behind closed doors there was a lot of yelling. And a lot of silence."

"It makes me wonder if anyone stays together anymore."

"You and your husband are still together."

"That's true," Caroline said, feeling more proud of this fact than she ever had.

Officer Dugan rounded the corner, carrying a white first-aid box in his hand. Barbara trailed him, arms folded.

"How's the head?" he asked.

"Okay, I guess," Caroline said. "It doesn't hurt, if that's what you mean."

"Head wounds bleed a lot," Dugan said. "They often look worse than they really are. I'm just going to put a bandage on it for now."

After several attempts to tape sterile gauze to the wound, Dugan finally took out a roll of gauze and wrapped it around her head in order to hold the bandage in place.

"Damn, you look like someone brained you," Emily said.

"I brained myself," Caroline said. "Is this really necessary?"

"Yes," Dugan said. "No arguments."

"And?" Barbara Kingman said.

Dugan looked to Caroline and Emily and rolled his eyes. "Would you mind apologizing to Mrs. Kingman for trespassing on her property?"

"Oh, come on," Emily said.

"No, it's fine," Caroline said. "You've done enough apologizing for one day." She turned to Barbara Kingman. "I'm sorry, Mrs. Kingman. We didn't mean any harm."

"Try harder next time," she said.

A minute later, Dugan was helping Caroline into her car. "I don't blame the lady," he said. "Kids are in that tree house constantly. She must call us twice a month. And if the kids see us coming, which they usually do, they bolt into those woods behind the house and it's damn near impossible to catch them."

"She's still a bitch," Emily said.

"I won't argue with that," Dugan said. "I'll follow you back to your mom's. See if Polly's shown up there yet. Call off the dogs."

Emily turned to Caroline. "You mind if I go with you back to your mom's house? I want to see this through with you. Make sure Polly's safe and sound."

"Sure," Caroline said. Then she smiled. "But I can't guarantee that she'll be nice to you when we find her."

"That's okay," Emily said. "I deserve it."

Tom tensed at the sight of the cruiser pulling into Penelope's driveway.

"It's fine, Tom," Caroline said, climbing out of her own car.

"Oh my God!" Tom said, moving quickly to close the gap between them. "What happened?"

"Nothing," Caroline said. "He's just here to see if Polly made it home yet."

"I'm talking about your head," he said, motioning to her forehead.

"Oh, God. I forgot. I hit my head on a beam."

"Are you okay?" he asked, leaning in to get a closer look.

"Yeah, I'm fine."

"Jesus. You're covered in blood. Are you sure?"

"She's fine," Dugan said. "You can take her to the hospital if you'd like. Better safe than sorry. But I don't think there's any concussion, and I'm pretty sure it's stopped bleeding."

"How did you hit your head on a beam?" Tom asked.

"In a tree house. It's a long story. Any word from Polly?"

"No," Tom said, shaking his head. "I just pulled in. I went to

White Hen and the diner and that plaza down the street. I thought she might be hanging out somewhere, nursing a coffee. You didn't find anything either?"

"I did," Caroline said, remembering her possibly good news. "Charleston Chew wrappers and Red Bull. Looks like Polly stayed in my old tree house last night. But she'd left already by the time we got there."

Tom looked relieved. "At least we know she's okay."

"Are you guys still looking for Polly?" All four heads turned to the porch, where Agnes was sitting in the rocking chair that had been occupied by Spartacus the day before.

"Yes?" Caroline said.

"She's in the backyard," Agnes said.

"What?"

"She's in the backyard," Agnes repeated.

"What's she doing in the backyard?" Tom asked.

"Attending a funeral," Agnes said, as if it were the most natural thing in the world.

twenty-six

George Durrow and Polly were standing shoulder to shoulder amongst the tiny markers that dotted the backyard lawn. Spartacus was standing a couple paces to their left. They were facing Penelope Waters, who was dressed in what appeared to be a black robe and holding an open book in her hands. A small, rectangular hole and a tiny pile of dirt filled the space between them. Caroline could tell that she was speaking, but the combination of the roar of the river and the distance between them prevented the words from making their way to her.

"It's okay," Tom said, placing his hand on her shoulder. "We can just wait inside."

"No," Caroline said.

"Are you sure?" Tom asked.

Emily, flanking Caroline on the opposite side, gave a quizzical look. "What's wrong?"

"Caroline doesn't—," Tom began.

"I haven't been to a funeral since my sister died."

"Oh," Emily said.

"Listen," Tom said, adopting his ministerial tone. "Maybe this isn't the time—"

"It's exactly the time." As she crossed the lawn and navigated her way through the rows of tiny headstones, Caroline thought back on Lucy's funeral, a memory she had been avoiding for more than two decades. It had been a day similar to today: clear skies, light breeze, sun high in the sky. Caroline's uncle Bill had driven Caroline and her mother over in his paneled station wagon. The car had been full of adult passengers, which meant that Caroline had to sit alone in the way-back, a space that in today's seatbelt culture was reserved for luggage and pets. No one spoke during the ten-minute drive. The only sound was the near-silent wailing of her mother.

Caroline hated the birds that day. She was standing between her mother and her aunt June at the grave site, squinting at the sun's glare as it reflected off the polished wooden surface of the casket. Lucy was inside that small box, she knew. Cold, lifeless Lucy, the little girl who wanted nothing more than to be just like her big sister. Lucy was going to be lowered into the ground and buried forever, and yet the birds continued to chirp and sing in the trees around them as the moment drew near, oblivious to the fact that the world had been cracked in two.

Caroline had been trapped in a space between grief and terror. The weight of the sadness over the loss of Lucy was unbearable, and yet there was also the ever-present fear that someone would discover that she was responsible for her sister's death. That everyone would hate her as much as she hated herself.

Another bird, she thought, spotting the wooden box in George's right hand as she drew near the small gathering.

Her mother's eyes were focused on the book in her hands. Caroline had initially thought it was the Bible, but now that she was closer, it looked too thin. Her mother had just turned a page and begun reading when her words finally carried over the sound of the river. It was a poem, and one Caroline knew well.

> *Our revels are now ended. These our actors,*
> *As I foretold you, were all spirits and*
> *Are melted into air, into thin air:*
> *And like the baseless fabric of this vision,*
> *The cloud-capp'd towers, the gorgeous palaces,*
> *The solemn temples, the great globe itself,*

Yea all which it inherit, shall dissolve
And, like this insubstantial pageant faded,
Leave not a rack behind. We are such stuff
As dreams are made on, and our little life
Is rounded in a sleep

Tears welled up in her eyes.

A second later, her mother asked for a moment of silence.

Caroline came alongside Polly and touched her arm lightly. Polly turned. Her eyes widened as she focused in on her mother's forehead. Caroline quickly shook her head in an attempt to dismiss Polly's concern. "It's okay," she said, mouthing the words, not wanting to disturb this moment of silence. "Don't worry. It's nothing."

"What the hell happened to you?" Penelope was staring at her daughter. A second later George was, too.

"Are you all right?" he asked.

"Who?" Spartacus asked, turning in her general direction.

"I'm fine," she said. "Honestly. I banged my head. That's all. I'm here for support. Just keep going, Mom."

"Then why are you crying?" Polly asked.

"Who's crying?" Spartacus asked.

"Caroline," her mother said. "Caroline's crying."

"It's just a bird," Spartacus said. "No offense, George."

Caroline wiped her eyes with the sleeve of her shirt. "Please. Don't let me interrupt."

"We're almost done," her mother said. "Are you sure you want to be here?"

"She's sure."

Polly and Caroline turned to see Emily, Tom, and Officer Dugan.

It was Emily who had spoken.

Caroline's mother managed a smile before turning her head back down to the book. "All right, let's continue then. The final reading of the afternoon will be by my granddaughter, Polly Jacobs."

"Not exactly a reading," Polly said. "Just some stuff that I wanted to say."

Caroline's mother looked to George. "It's okay," he said. "I'm sure that whatever she says will be perfect."

Penny stepped aside. Polly took her spot in front of the small gathering. "There's a company in England that will send professional mourners to your funeral, so you can look more popular than you really were."

"Is that true?" Spartacus asked.

"Shush," Penny said. "Let her speak."

"She can tell me later," Spartacus said.

"Shush!"

"It's okay," Polly said. "And yes, it's true. I think it's kind of amazing that some people need to hire professional mourners for their funerals, and we have so many people here today for Tutu's funeral."

"Amen," Penelope whispered.

Spartacus nodded.

George sniffled.

"They say that death is hardest on the living," Polly said, louder now. More official. "But whoever said that was an idiot. A total moron. And whoever said it was alive at the time, so he was hardly in the position to know. I don't know if a man said it, but I think it's a safe assumption. Sounds like something a guy would say."

Polly paused for a moment, seeming to lose her place. She looked up at Caroline. Took a deep breath and found her place again.

"No, I say that death is hardest on the dead, because death sucks. It's the reason why we don't step in front of buses or jump off bridges. It's why we're not supposed to go gentle into that good night. Death is the worst. It steals everything. It makes everything important unimportant. It makes hard work meaningless. It steals friendship and love."

"Polly," her grandmother said. "That's enough."

"No, it's okay," George said between sniffles. "Go on."

"We may all grieve the loss of Tutu—some more than others—

but we can all go on with the memory of Tutu in our hearts. For us, there is still stuff ahead. Beauty and love. Laughter and smiles. We can carry Tutu in our hearts wherever we go, and someday the sadness that we feel about her death will be replaced by happy memories and nostalgia. But for Tutu, there will be no more sunny days. No more love or joy. Her book is closed. Never to be opened again. We stand here today to mourn the loss of Tutu. But do not mourn for your loss. Mourn for hers. We still have the bright and happy memory of Tutu to carry us forward. She has nothing."

Spartacus wiped away tears from his eyes. "I never even knew Tutu."

Caroline's mother squeezed his arm.

"Oh," Polly said, the formality of her voice now gone. "Unless of course you believe in heaven, and in this case, a heaven for birds. If that's the case, then Tutu is probably nibbling on a mountain of birdseed right now, happier than all of us. But honestly, who believes in heaven anymore?"

"*Polly!*" Caroline's mother said.

"One more thing," Polly said. "Did you know that President Andrew Jackson's pet parrot had to be removed from his funeral because it wouldn't stop swearing? I think Tutu would've liked that."

By the time Polly had finished speaking, Caroline was crying.

"Don't worry," George said, reaching over and squeezing her hand. "Spartacus is right. Tutu was only a bird, and she lived a good, long life."

But Caroline barely heard George's words. She was thinking about Lucy and that day on the corner of Summer and Federal streets. The little girl a full head shorter than she, always looking up, always squinting into the sunlight, always smiling. The little girl who loved pancakes but despised waffles, who never met a set of stairs that she didn't run up, and who followed her big sister with a ferocity that bordered on obsession.

She was thinking about that girl and the terrible, awful moment that ended it all.

Fifteen minutes later, Caroline was sitting on the front porch in the rocking chair. She had asked to be left alone for a while, though she wasn't sure why. The floodgates had opened on her memories of the day Lucy had died, but the memories had always been there, pushing and nudging and constantly threatening to creep into her consciousness. Tutu's funeral had given rise to them. She felt foolish and weak sitting in the rocking chair, red faced and teary-eyed. She had wanted to stand beside her daughter at the funeral for a dead bird. She had wanted to dispense with this burden once and for all. Instead, she had fallen apart.

"Caroline?" It was George, stepping out onto the porch. "I have to go, but I just wanted to say thank you."

Caroline smiled. "For what? Ruining the funeral?"

"Ruining it? I thought I was going to be alone back there. Then Polly showed up, which was amazing, and she guilted Spartacus into joining us. And then you and your husband and your friend and the police officer showed up. I only wish Tutu could've seen how many people were there." He snickered a little and then added, "Actually, I wish my family could've seen how many people came. They thought the whole thing was ridiculous."

"Still, I'm sorry for all the tears, "Caroline said. "It was a little over the top." She didn't have the heart to tell him that the tears she had wept for a long dead sister and not for Tutu.

"It was a funeral," he said. "Tears are mandatory."

Caroline rose from the chair and reached out to hug George. "I'm sorry for your loss. I really am."

"I know. Thanks."

Caroline stood on the edge of the porch, watching as George climbed into his car and backed out of the driveway. Two days ago she had thought that he was a strange little man. She wasn't entirely wrong, but George Durow had proved to be so much more as well.

Polly seemed to have known it all along.

"I assume you weren't bawling about the bird?" It was Polly.

She had sidled alongside Caroline in time to watch as George's car disappeared around the curve on Main Street and into a reddening sky.

"Mind telling me where you were all night?"

"The cop already told me that you found my hideout," Polly said. "Pretty clever."

"Then would you mind telling me why you ran away in the first place?"

"I didn't run away. I was just pissed at you and had no place to go. We're sharing a bedroom. Remember?"

"So you figured you'd stay away all night?"

"Sometimes I disappear to my room for days, in case you didn't notice. This was less than twenty-four hours. You should consider yourself lucky."

"I should consider myself lucky?"

For a second, it appeared as if Polly was going to fire back. Then she stopped. "Fine, I'm sorry. If it makes you feel any better, I froze my butt off last night."

"It doesn't. You scared the hell out of me. Out of all of us."

"I said I was sorry. And hey, I like your photos. You got them back, right?"

"Yeah, I did. You do?"

"They're really good, Mom. I kind of love them. You should put them online. Let people see them."

"There's a big difference between your family liking your work and the world liking your work."

"No kidding," Polly said. "The world can't like anything you do if you never let them see it."

"Someday. I'm just not ready yet."

"Are you trying to be the next Grandma Moses?"

"I'm not that old," Caroline said.

"Not yet," Polly said. "But if you wait long enough, you might find yourself old and gray before anyone sees your stuff. Seriously, Mom. It's time to stop hiding behind your camera. You're actually talented. It's shocking but true."

"Don't think this is getting you out of trouble for last night."

"Hey, I have an idea," Polly said. She was trying to change the subject, Caroline knew. "Ever hear of J D Wetherspoon?"

"No."

"It's this chain of British pubs. Like nine hundred of them altogether, owned by this guy named Tim Martin. Guess where he got the name for the pubs."

"I'm guessing he didn't name them after himself," Caroline said.

"No, he named them after a teacher who told him that he'd never be successful in business. Don't you love that? He named his business out of spite. And revenge."

"And, my Polymath?" Caroline said, knowing that there was more.

"I think you should open up that photography studio you've always wanted and name it something like Better Than Emily. Or Suck It, Emily Kaplan."

Caroline smiled.

The two stood on the porch in silence, watching the cars drive by, avoiding eye contact. Last night Caroline had been ready, anxious even, to tell Polly the secret that she had kept hidden for so long—both in her heart and in the closet in the upstairs bedroom of this house. It had felt so right. Almost meant to be. But now it felt as if the barriers between the two of them had been reestablished and to break through them would be impossible. Mother and daughter, opposing forces on the battlefield once again.

"So what were you crying about if it wasn't Tutu or your broken head?" Polly asked. "I was actually worried about you for a minute there."

And just like that, the door opened once again. Polly had extended her hand, absent of sarcasm and malice, and all Caroline had to do was grab it.

twenty-seven

It was exactly as she had remembered: the pink and yellow bed-spread, the misshapen beanbag chair, the enormous stuffed panda slumped in the corner, the heart-shaped mirror above the dresser. All seemed ancient and innocent. Frozen in time. Even the dusty light filtering in through pink curtains felt nostalgic. As far as Caroline knew, nothing had been touched since the day that Lucy had died. She knew that her mother occasionally spent time in this room, sitting on the window seat or the edge of Lucy's bed, and she would dust and vacuum on rare occasions, but otherwise it had been undisturbed, a monument to a sister who had been gone for so long.

"I've never seen the inside of this room before," Polly said, peering over her mother's shoulder.

The last time Caroline had been in here, she had stuffed a plastic bag in the back of Lucy's closet. She had been panicked and frightened and consumed with guilt. Her hands had trembled as she reached back into the closet as far as she could. Standing here now, on the edge of the past, she understood the enormity of the guilt she'd carried with her through her life. It had become a part of her, as essential as her heart and lungs. It was what made her who she was. Caroline was here to share her most secret of secrets with her daughter, but she now understood that doing so would not alleviate her guilt. That could never happen.

"When was the last time you were in here?" Polly asked.

"I haven't seen this room since I was your age," Caroline said. "God, it looks exactly the same."

"Are we going in?"

Three small steps and Caroline reached the purple rug that filled the center of the room. She turned slowly, taking in the entirety of the space as she did. Beside the bed was a small desk and chair. Caroline stepped over to it. *Adventures in Mathematics,* a textbook that she had once used in elementary school, was sitting atop a dictionary and a Nancy Drew mystery. Beside the books was a spiral bound notebook, a small diary with a tiny padlock, and a ceramic bowl full of hair elastics, barrettes, and ribbons. Lucy had made the bowl at summer camp. Caroline knew that if she turned it over, she would find Lucy's initials carved roughly in the bottom.

She took a step closer and saw strands of hair wrapped around a couple of elastics. It seemed eerie that parts of Lucy still existed in this room where time had stopped.

"What's this?" Polly asked, speaking in a soft, reverent voice.

She turned. Polly was standing by the bedside table and pointing at a small pile of yellow and black Memorex cassette tapes. "Those are Lucy's tapes," Caroline said, stepping over for a closer look. "I'd forgotten all about them. She got a tape recorder for Christmas one year, and she would spend hours recording songs off the radio while she sang to them. Kind of like old school karaoke."

"She'd hold the tape recorder up to the radio?" Polly asked.

"It was a different time," Caroline said. "Lucy loved to sing to the radio. Madonna. Whitney Houston. The Bangles."

"Madonna was making music when you were a kid?"

"Are you kidding me? Madonna's been around—"

"I was kidding," Polly said.

"Ha-ha."

"Is it okay if I sit?" Polly asked.

"Sure. On the window seat. Okay?"

Caroline remained standing in the center of the room. She stared at the bed and could almost see her sister snuggled under the covers, propped up on a pile of pillows, listening to the radio and reading a book.

Lucy had been the best person that Caroline had ever known. She was kind and unrelentingly happy. And she had died before the temptations of life could pierce her childhood innocence. Lucy never had the chance to take a drag on her first cigarette or steal a pair of cheap earrings from the pharmacy or let a boy slide his hand down her pants in the backseat of a car. She had read her mystery stories and listened to her music and finished her home-work before dinner each day. And then one day she took the last bike ride of her life.

Caroline was crying before she realized it, sobbing uncontrol-lably, and before she could say a word, Polly had taken her by the hand and was pulling her toward the window seat.

"No," Caroline said. "Wait."

"What?"

"Just wait."

Caroline took a deep breath between sobs, trying to bring them under control, and then stepped over to the other side of the room. She opened the closet door. The smell of cedar instantly filled her nostrils, making the past seem even more real than a moment ago.

"What is it, Mom?" Polly asked, and for some reason, hear-ing Polly say *Mom* was enough to bring the sobbing back. She took another deep breath, wiped the tears from her face and eyes, and then got down on her hands and knees. She crawled into the closet, ducking underneath long forgotten cotton dresses and a yellow terrycloth bathrobe, and reached into the back corner of the closet. She felt around, worried for a moment by the empty space, and then her fingertips felt the plastic. She pulled, careful to grasp the bag by the handles so the contents wouldn't spill. A second later, she was holding the very thing that she had avoided thinking about and yet somehow never stopped thinking about for the last twenty-five years.

"What is it?" Polly asked. Her voice was still soft. Caroline hadn't told her why she had been brought here, but Polly seemed to know that it was something important.

"It's . . . ," Caroline said, unsure of her next words, not because she was choosing them carefully but because she didn't know what to say. Didn't know how to describe the benign yet life-altering contents of the bag. Instead, she stepped over to the window seat and sat down beside Polly, plastic bag in her lap.

"It's okay, Mom. Seriously." Polly put her arm around Caroline, and instantly she dipped her face into her daughter's shoulder and began to weep. She had never wept so hard in her life.

Caroline wasn't sure how long she cried in Polly's arms, but the moment finally came when she was able to breathe without sobs and blink without tears. She gave her daughter a final squeeze and straightened.

"Are you all right?" Polly asked.

"Apparently not," Caroline said, wiping her eyes again but managing a smile.

"Maybe we should get out of here."

"No, I have something to show you. And tell you."

"You don't need to," Polly said. "Not if you don't want to."

"No. I want to." Caroline opened the bag and pulled out a black shirt and handed it to Polly.

"What?" she asked, turning it over in her hands.

"Take a look."

Polly unfolded the shirt and held it up. It was a short-sleeve black concert T-shirt with THE RAMONES emblazoned across the top in block letters. Below it was the image of the band's four members, standing side by side, sort of leaning on one another.

"Cool shirt," Polly said. "I didn't know you were into The Ramones."

"I'm not," Caroline said. "I mean, I wasn't."

"It's Aunt Lucy's?"

It always sounded odd when Polly referred to Lucy as her aunt. But here in this room, in this time, it seemed absurd. She was already older than Lucy had ever been. Polly was growing and changing every day, but Lucy was frozen in time, a little girl forever.

"No," she said. "Not Lucy's. It's mine."

"I don't get it."

Caroline pulled a similar shirt from the bag and held it up. This one had a list of the 1986 tour dates for Echo & the Bunnymen listed on the back and the band's name scribbled across the front. Caroline stared at the shirt, recalling the moment when she had chosen it from a rack full of similar shirts. She had spent so much time at that rack, examining each shirt before finally making a decision, as if choosing the right one might change her fate.

In many ways, she suddenly realized, it had. If she hadn't spent fifteen minutes going back and forth between this shirt and three others, weighing the advantages of each, things might've turned out very differently for her and Lucy. This thought had never occurred to her until just now, and it only served to add to the immense weight of her guilt. She had the sudden desire to use this time machine of a bedroom to shout back at that fifteen-year-old version of herself, to tell her that the damn shirt didn't matter, that it wouldn't have mattered even if she had all of the Echo & the Bunnymen shirts that ever existed. She wanted desperately to tell that earlier version of herself that you can't restore a friendship with the right T-shirt.

"Mom?" Polly said. "Are you all right?"

"I bought these shirts on the day Lucy died."

Polly sat still, eyebrows slightly raised, waiting for more. Had she spoken, asked a question or made comment, Caroline thought that she might've changed the subject and avoided everything that came next. Taken the easy road. But Polly either knew that it was important to remain silent or didn't know what to say.

"My mother had a rule," Caroline finally said. "Lucy was only allowed to ride her bike to the end of Federal Street. Main Street, because it had sidewalks, and Federal Street, because it was a quiet road. Lucy was allowed to ride up the hill to the stop sign, but that was as far as she could go. I could ride my bike anywhere I wanted, and I did, but all Lucy ever wanted to do was follow me, so I had to either ride up and down Main and Federal with her all day or leave her behind. So I left her behind a lot, and sometimes it was fine because either she was busy doing something else, and sometimes she just annoyed the hell out of me and I had to get away for a while. But a lot of the time I hated leaving her behind. She'd stop her bike at the end of Federal Street and cry as I rode off, and it broke my heart.

"Then that thing with Emily happened in the cafeteria, and I didn't know what to do. I hid in the library during lunch for the rest of the week, but I finally decided that I needed to do something to get Emily back. That's when I decided that I had to become cooler than I was. I figured that I'd lost Emily because Ellie was cooler than me, so if I could . . . you know, be more like Ellie, I could get my seat back at the lunch table, or at least convince them to let me drag a chair over to the table. I know. It sounds ridiculous."

"No, it doesn't," Polly said. "Not at all. I've spent half my life trying to be cool."

Caroline smiled. She didn't think this was true, but she loved Polly for saying it.

"I knew I needed to start liking the right music. I thought that would be my way in. So on that Saturday morning, I decided to ride my bike to Strawberries."

"Strawberries?" Polly asked.

"A music store. It was popular when I was growing up. Back when you didn't buy music on the Internet. There was a Strawberries in Bellingham, just one town over from Blackstone. Not very far from here, even."

"Grandma couldn't drive you?" Polly asked.

"No. I mean, she could've, but she was a mess back then. We were barely talking. And I didn't want her to know what I was doing. I was embarrassed about myself. You know what I mean? I was trying to hide until I could make a better version of myself."

"That happens all the time," Polly said. "Kids are always trying to make themselves into something new."

Caroline was on a roll now. "And besides," she said. "Strawberries wasn't that far away. I used to ride my bike everywhere. It wasn't like it is today. We could disappear for the day and never tell our parents where we went. I figured that I'd ride my bike to the store, spend my allowance on a couple punk albums, and then be home before lunch. It was early in the morning, maybe nine, and I wanted to leave before Lucy noticed me taking off. She was eating cereal and watching Saturday morning cartoons, so I thought I could sneak away. But as I was riding my bike down the driveway, she came running out of house, shoes untied, Cheerios still stuck to her shirt, screaming my name. I almost ignored her. For one split second, I thought about pretending that I didn't hear her and just riding away."

Caroline paused for a moment, realizing how close she had come to changing everything that was to follow. If she had just ignored Lucy like she had wanted, everything would be different.

"But she was yelling my name," Caroline said, pressing on. "Screaming it. Crying it out, really. And in that split second, I remembered the way Emily had just walked away from me in the cafeteria and how I'd felt being left behind. So I stopped.

"She told me to wait up. That's what she used to say all the time. *Wait up.* 'Let me get my bike,' she said. So I told her that I was going past Federal Street but I promised to ride with her when I got back. But she said she still wanted to go. Just as far as Federal Street, she said, so I agreed. But when we got to the end of Federal Street, she started crying. Asking me to stay. Asking me to ride with her just a little bit more. And when I said no, that's when she asked if she could come with me. She'd never asked that before. She'd always thought of everything past Federal Street as no-man's-land. But for some reason, Lucy chose that day to get brave. And she promised that she wouldn't tell Mom if I let her, and she promised not to be a PITA."

Polly scrunched her eyebrows in confusion. "PITA?"

"Pain in the ass. It's what I called Lucy when she was annoying me. She promised to listen to me and not get in the way. She begged and begged and I finally said yes. I let her come with me. All the way to Bellingham. And when we got to Strawberries, she was the one who talked me into T-shirts instead of music. She said I could always find the songs on the radio, and she would record them for me on her tape recorder. But the T-shirts were way cooler. That's how she said it. 'Way cooler.'

"On the way home, she was getting tired. She wasn't used to riding so far. She was struggling up the hills and had to walk her bike up a steep one on Elm Street. I tried to go slow so she could keep up. I even rode behind her for a while on that road with Log Cabin Pizza, just so I could keep an eye on her because of all the traffic. Then she fell behind, and I didn't watch her carefully enough, and—"

"It's okay, Mom. You don't have to say any more."

"Yes, Polly. I do." Caroline took a deep breath and continued. "I didn't watch my little sister carefully enough and she got hit by that car and was killed. Killed right in front of me. In the same spot where I agreed to let her break the rule and come along. All I had to do was say *no.* I'd said it a million times before. A billion times before. All I had to do was tell her to go home and watch *Super Friends* and wait for me. If I'd done that, Lucy would be alive today."

Caroline had thought about these things before, but until this moment, she had never said any of them aloud. She had hoped that doing so would alleviate some of her guilt. Release her from her secret. Maybe even come to the realization that it was crazy to blame herself after so many years. But it just made everything more real. Made her guilt seem even more justified. She had broken her mother's rule, and as a result, her little sister was dead. She'd been dead for twenty-five years. But somehow, in this room, in this moment, it was as if Lucy had died all over again.

"So you've been blaming yourself since the day Aunt Lucy died?" Polly asked. "'Cause that's crazy, Mom. You were just a kid."

"I don't believe that, and you don't, either."

"How do you know what I believe?"

"You said it yourself," Caroline said. "There's no bright red line between childhood and adulthood. We are who we are. Emily is still the bitch from the high school cafeteria, and I'm still the big sister who got her little sister killed on Summer Street."

"Bullshit," Polly said. There was real anger in her voice, and it caught Caroline off guard. "What happened to Lucy was an accident. There was no way of knowing that she would get killed. The only thing you're guilty of is bad luck."

"My mother made a rule to keep Lucy safe. I broke it."

"No," Polly said. "That's stupid. Do you have any idea how many times kids break rules? I break them every day. Am I supposed to be worried that every time Kate and I don't use the crosswalk, Kate might get run over by a bus and I'll end up blaming myself for her death?"

"You're not responsible for Kate. I was responsible for Lucy."

"No," Polly said, her voice at a near shout. "You were fifteen. You weren't even responsible for yourself."

Caroline opened her mouth to speak but Polly cut her off.

"Do you know how stupid this whole thing is? We're sitting here in your dead sister's bedroom, arguing about whether or not it's your fault that she's dead, and you sound like a crazy person. Every single person on the planet would agree with me. But you're sitting here, dripping tears on perfectly good vintage T-shirts, blaming yourself for something that isn't your fault. When you're fifteen, you're allowed to make stupid mistakes. You're supposed to make stupid mistakes. Even if they turn out terrible. But when you're forty, you're not supposed to be this stupid."

Caroline found herself with the simultaneous urge to ground her daughter for a month and hug her as tightly as possible.

"I'm sorry," Polly said, her voice returning to its reverent state. "But I'm right. You're acting like a complete idiot."

"Even if you're right, and I'm not saying that you are, do you think that I can just erase a lifetime of guilt in five minutes?"

"Yeah, I do. Just decide that you're an idiot, and you're not going to be an idiot anymore. It's not that hard. Look at Grandma. You said she was a disaster when you were a kid. Now look at her."

"She didn't change overnight, either."

"Yeah, but you're a lot smarter than Grandma."

Caroline smiled. "I wish it could be as easy as you think. Things always seem a lot easier when you're young."

"They always seem a lot more complicated when you get old."

Mother and daughter sat in silence for a minute, each staring down at the shirt in their hands.

Finally, Polly spoke. "If you're going to keep blaming yourself, why did you bring me here in the first place?"

"I thought that telling someone might make it easier to live with."

"Did it?"

"Maybe it has. Or it will."

"Good," Polly said with finality. "You should tell Dad, too."

"You think?"

"Yeah. He's good with that stuff. He's a pain in the ass when you don't actually have a problem, but when you do, he's good to have around. And he won't call you names like I did. And he's your husband. He should know." She paused and then added, "But don't tell Grandma."

"No?"

"No way," Polly said. "She's a total drama queen. She'd find a way to make it about her."

Caroline now understood why she brought her daughter along on this adventure. It had nothing to do with Emily Kaplan-turned-Labonte. It had everything to do with this moment.

twenty-eight

There were fewer people around the table this time. George Durrow was absent, of course, as were Spartacus and Agnes. Spartacus (with Agnes by his side) had played in a poker tournament the night before and had begged off in favor of sleeping in.

Jake and Randy were also not present. "Fishing," Emily had said, though for some reason Caroline didn't think she was telling the truth.

The only addition to the table was Tom. She was glad that he was here.

"Don't worry," Polly said to Emily as she stepped into the room. "Plenty of seats this time. I promise."

"Good to know," Emily said.

Caroline knew that Polly's pleasantries were not to be confused with actual friendliness or even tacit approval of her presence at this meal. Despite their "come to Jesus" moment in Lucy's bedroom—as Polly was now referring to it—she was still angry about Caroline's civility toward Emily.

"After all that you've been through these last couple days, you still can't tell her to fuck off?"

"I did," Caroline said. "Or I came as close to it as I needed to. That's the difference between adults and teenagers. Adults don't see everything as black and white. Also, we're allowed to swear and you're not, so knock it off."

"That's the problem with the world," Polly said. "Adults make everything so complicated. Sometimes a bully is nothing more than a bully."

She wasn't going to tell Polly that she was right, but the girl had a point.

Caroline's mother was serving eggs, bacon, and pancakes this time. Brunch before she and Polly and Tom made their return trip home.

"It's kind of like old times," Penelope said to Emily as she passed a serving dish of scrambled eggs across the table. "Do you remember all those mornings you spent at our old place as a kid, eating breakfast with us?'

"I do," Emily said. "Some of my favorite childhood memories were made in that house. I hated it when you guys had to move."

"Me, too," Caroline's mother said.

"Why did you move?" Jane asked.

Caroline saw her mother hesitate for a second and rushed to fill the gap. "My father took a drive to Florida and never came back. Mom did an amazing job taking care of us."

"Us?" Jane asked.

This time it was Caroline who faltered, so Polly quickly jumped in. "My aunt Lucy. She died when she was still a kid. Grandma was like some kind of superhero. Dealing with all that."

"I'm so sorry," Jane said. "I didn't know."

"It's all right," Penelope said. "Long time ago. Many days since then. We still miss her, but we've come a long way."

We have come a long way, Caroline thought. And in that moment, as she came a little bit closer to accepting the random nature of her sister's death, Caroline thought of what Polly had said. And she supposed that she had somehow understood it all along. If you nudge an asteroid off course by just a tiny bit and give it enough time, it will end up in an entirely different place. Life is no different. Nudge someone one way or the next and a person's life trajectory can change forever. The events of the last few days were the direct result of a moment in a cafeteria a long time ago. A small act of cruelty made large by time. Caroline couldn't blame Emily for Lucy's death, even though it was Emily who had set things in motion that day so very long ago.

But Polly was also wrong, because unlike the asteroid, which floats through the void on a specific trajectory, there is no predetermined course for a human life. No intended destination. Emily might have nudged her life off course years ago, but had Caroline not been so hell-bent on winning her friend back, things could've turned out very different. It didn't make what Emily did any less cruel. Just less profound.

And even though she would've given anything to have Lucy back, Caroline had more than enough reasons to feel fortunate about where life had brought her. The accumulation of decisions and choices and random acts had led her to this place and this time, and it wasn't all bad. She had a husband who she loved dearly. She had a daughter who she had grown to like as well as love, and someone whom she admired. Somewhere along the way, Polly had become Polly. Her own person. Not some hybrid version of her mother and father, as was the case for so many children, but her own self. Unlike anything Tom or Caroline were or could ever be.

Had her life been different, there might have been no Polly, and that would've been just as terrible as no Lucy.

"Maybe when you come back, we can do this at our place," Emily said.

"That would be great," Tom said. "We should probably make an effort to visit more often."

"I've been telling my parents that for years," Polly said.

"Yeah, we should," Caroline said. She was surprised by these words, but they felt right. She had avoided this place for so long, but now it felt . . . better. Not exactly good, but not awful, either. Just a place filled with memories. Some terrible, but some good ones, too. She hadn't seen the good ones in a long time, but they had begun to peek out from the thawing ground like spring's first flowers.

An hour later, they were saying their good-byes. Emily and Caroline were standing on the front porch, watching as Tom loaded what little luggage they had acquired during the trip into the trunk of his car.

"I feel like I should say more," Emily said. "Like good-bye isn't enough."

"We've said more than enough. For now, at least."

"So this isn't good-bye forever?" Emily asked.

Caroline laughed. "I don't think so. Not if you don't want it to be. I'm not saying that we're going to be best friends again, but I'll at least save you a seat at the table."

Emily reached out and hugged Caroline. They held each other for a long moment. Caroline breathed in and caught the smell of Emily's hair and skin. So many things had changed, but somehow, underneath everything, the past still lived and breathed as well.

"Enough, already," Polly said, exiting the house and walking past the two women. "Get a freaking room." Polly walked over to Emily's car and knocked on the window. Jane lowered it.

"I just wanted to say I'm sorry that I was such a bitch to you."

"It's okay," Jane said.

Then Polly leaned her head into the window, said something that Caroline couldn't hear, and stepped away.

"Ready?" Tom asked.

"Yup," Caroline said. She turned back to Emily. "If you need to talk, call me."

"I will," Emily said. Caroline thought she would. Sooner than later. She wondered if Emily regretted the loss of her friend as much as Caroline had.

"Sorry for everything," Polly said to Emily, who had stepped down off the porch with Caroline. "But not really."

"Polly!" Caroline said.

"It's fine," Emily said. "Is there anything better than a daughter who is willing to defend her mother to the end?"

Caroline thought not.

She got into her car and put the key into the ignition. The passenger-side door opened. Polly climbed in.

"You're not driving with Dad?" Caroline asked.

"Maybe I'll switch when we stop for lunch."

"Are you sure?" Caroline asked.

"Yeah. We need to talk. I can't end up as the next Max Brod."

"Who?"

Polly sighed. "*Max Brod.* The guy who promised Kafka that he would burn all of his unpublished manuscripts when he died."

"And did he?" Caroline asked.

"Are you kidding me?

"Fine," Caroline said. "He didn't burn them. What does that have to do with you?"

"You and Kafka are a lot alike. A couple of talented cowards. Actually, I think Kafka's overrated. That giant cockroach story is a joke. But you? You might be the real deal, Mom. If you'd ever let someone see your work. I don't want to be showing people those spider photos after you're dead. You need to find some eyeballs now."

"And you're going to make that happen?"

"It's called the Internet," Polly said. "I'll explain on the way."

"Sounds good," Caroline said. And it did. "But I get to listen to my music."

Caroline shifted the car into reverse and started backing out. "Sorry. It's fifty-fifty in this car. Your mother is no pushover."

"Relax, Mom. You're not exactly Helen of Troy yet." She was silent for a moment, and then she added, "But you're a lot less Neville Chamberlain than I thought you were."

Caroline wasn't sure who Neville Chamberlain was, but she assumed it was a compliment. She'd double check later on the Internet. "By the way," she said. "What did you say to Jane? When you stuck your head through her window?"

"I told her that her mother was a hamster and her father smelt of elderberries."

"Did she know what that meant?

"Nope," Polly said with a giggle. "She just stared at me."

"What does it mean?" Caroline asked.

Polly sighed. "It means that you and I are going to sit down in the living room tonight and watch *Monty Python and the Holy Grail*, so you'll stop asking such dumb questions."

That sounded just fine to Caroline.

Acknowledgments

Stephen King suggests writing the first draft of your novel with the door closed.

I suspect that Mr. King, whom I respect a great deal, did not spend his youth toiling away in the dim confines of an arcade or sitting in front of a television with an Atari 5200 controller in hand. Videogame junkies become hooked on immediate feedback and require it constantly. Though I have overcome my addiction and play sparingly nowadays, the need for immediate feedback never left me.

As a result, I write every sentence with the door open. In the process of completing this novel, I invited about a dozen friends and family members to read along as I wrote. While their helpful suggestions, generous praise, and private counsel were critical to my success, the most important thing was the knowledge that someone was reading and anxiously waiting for the next chapter.

For that, I am forever grateful.

Special thanks to my wife, Elysha, who gave me the idea for this story during one of our frequent conversations in bed with the lights out. Finding a best friend whom you constantly want to kiss is a wondrous thing.

Thanks to my in-laws, Barbara and Gerry Green, for continuing to fill my life with their enthusiasm, excitement, and unsolicited counsel. About once a month, Gerry will say, "Tell us something exciting, Matt! Give us some news!" He has no idea how long I have waited for someone to ask me questions like that.

Many thanks to Brenda Copeland, my editor and friend, for helping me find this story. From an awkward hand hold two years ago to our recent bout of smugness, she is a partner whom I never take for granted.

Lastly, thanks to Taryn Fagerness, my agent and friend, who makes my creative life possible. She makes my stories better and, as a result, my life better. Our relationship is the envy of so many of my author friends, and I brag about it whenever I can.

1. Caroline's meek personality is presented as a disadvantage, but do you think there are advantages to her temperament?

2. Would Caroline's photography be different if she were more assertive?

3. So much has changed since Caroline was in high school—but is it really so different now?

4. Today, we are much more aware of what constitutes bullying. Do you think student behavior has changed as a result?

5. What are the limits of spousal support? Is Caroline justified in asking Tom to simply trust her decision to drive to Massachusetts with their daughter?

6. When Polly lies to the hotel personnel to get an upgrade for their room, Caroline feels a sense of pride in her daughter. Is what Polly did acceptable? Is she being assertive or simply rude?

7. Are you the same person you were in high school? Do the choices made in youth reflect the person you will grow up to be?

8. How much of Polly's character is shaped by her parents' lack of assertiveness? Is it surprising that she would turn out to be different than her mother and father?

9. How has Caroline's guilt affected her photography career?

10. The author, Matthew Dicks, is a teacher; in what ways do you think this has influenced his portrayal of school politics?

11. Does the metaphor of the meteor slowly moving off course work? Can life be significantly altered by single events or is it more of a series of small events?

St. Martin's
Griffin